THE
HALF
LIFE
OF
MOLLY
PIERCE

THE HALF LIFE OF MOLLY PIERCE

KATRINA LENO

HARPER TEEN
An Imprint of HarperCollinsPublishers

to my brothers:

for their unfailing

& unconditional

support

The epigraph on page v is from *The Letters of Vincent van Gogh*, translation copyright by Constable & Co., 1927, 1929.

HarperTeen is an imprint of HarperCollins Publishers.

Library of Congress Cataloging-in-Publication Data
Leno, Katrina.
    The half life of Molly Pierce / Katrina Leno. — First edition.
        pages   cm
    Summary: "Molly, a seventeen-year-old girl who suffers from dissociative identity disorder, has played host to Mabel, a completely distinct personality, for most her life. When Molly faces a crisis Mabel doesn't know she can handle, Mabel lets Molly in on her secrets"— Provided by publisher.
    ISBN 978-0-06-223118-5
    [1. Multiple personality—Fiction. 2. Dissociative disorders— Fiction.] I. Title.
PZ7.L5399Hal   2014   2013021511
[Fic]—dc23   CIP
                                                                          AC

Typography by Alison Klapthor
16 17 18 19 20   LP/RRDH   10 9 8 7 6 5 4 3 2 1
❖
First paperback edition, 2016

Now for the moment things appear to be going very badly with me, and this has been so for a considerable time already, and may continue so in the future for a while; but after everything has seemed to go wrong, there will perhaps come a time when things will go right. I do not count on it, perhaps it will never happen, but if there should come a change for the better, I would consider it so much gain, I would be contented, I would say: at last! you see *there was something after all*!

—from *The Letters of Vincent van Gogh*, edited by Mark Roskill

ONE.

There are long stretches where I don't remember anything.

I wake up in my car.

I'm driving, but I don't know where I'm driving to and
I don't know where I'm driving from.

But it's my car. And my things are in it.

I just don't know how I got here.

It's only been a couple hours. I remember what I put on
this morning and I'm wearing the same clothes. A pair of
black tights. Jean shorts, a tucked-in flowered shirt. A gray
sweater, worn and pilled. My favorite sweater.

The clock in my car doesn't work and I can't find my

cell phone, so I don't know what time it is. But it's still light out and it's October now, a warm October, and it must be around two or three. The sun goes down so early. Did I miss school again? Sometimes I miss school. What's the last thing I can remember? Ten o'clock? Eleven? History—I can remember history. We're studying the Second World War. I'm in precalculus. I can't remember calculus. I've been out since ten thirty, eleven.

I check my body for bruises, for cuts, pressing fingers into my stomach and arms, checking to make sure I'm okay. Sometimes I'm cut up all over and sometimes there are twigs and leaves in my hair and once I was halfway to New York, driving too fast, and I had to pull over to the side of the road and catch my breath and figure out where I could turn around.

I live in Massachusetts, by the shore. A town called Manchester-by-the-Sea. That's the whole name of the town. The people here, they get angry when the tourists abbreviate it. But we can call it Manchester.

It took me four hours to drive back. Two tanks of gas. I broke curfew by three hours and I was grounded the entire weekend. Grounded for something I can't even remember doing.

It started a year ago and I haven't told anyone about it, even though it's only gotten worse. I can't tell anyone about it because . . .

There are a lot of reasons.

I'm scared they'll think I'm crazy.

I'm scared they won't believe me.

I'm scared there's something really wrong with me.

And so far, I'm handling it. I'm dealing with it.

Usually it's no more than an hour or two and sometimes it's only ten minutes. Sometimes I'll be watching a TV show, and then I wake up standing in my backyard and the same TV show is still on. So I can catch the ending, which I guess is good. Although I have no idea what's happened up until then.

And apparently I don't do anything too obvious. Because I've been around people before and nobody ever seems to notice. Nobody except Hazel, really. But Hazel notices everything.

Hazel is my sister. She's thirteen. It's her and me and Clancy, our brother. He's fifteen, a sophomore. I'm Molly. I'm a senior. I'll be eighteen soon.

Clancy never notices anything.

But Hazel.

She's asked me about it.

I act like she's crazy, which is the easiest thing to do.

Once I asked her if I ever seemed different.

She said yes.

But it was in a way nobody else would ever notice.

I said, What do you mean?

She said if I was going to keep secrets from her, she was going to keep secrets from me.

It happens once a week, maybe. Every other week. Sometimes more.

I don't know what it means.

I've thought about it and . . .

It scares me.

It leaves me feeling sort of hopeless and unable to control my own body. We're supposed to be able to do at least that, right? To tell our feet to move and suddenly we're walking. To tell our arms to lift and our tongue to talk.

To tell our brains to remember.

To commit something to memory.

I think there's something wrong with me.

I mean . . .

I guess I know there's something wrong with me. There has to be.

I get these headaches. Migraines. Sometimes they're really bad; sometimes I have to stay home from school and I have to lie still in bed and keep the blinds closed and sometimes I throw up into the yellow mixing bowl my mom puts on the floor next to me.

My therapist says they're related to my "emotional difficulties."

Those are his words, not mine.

He also calls it depression.

I don't like calling it that.

My mother calls it my melancholy. But I don't like calling it that, either.

But it's something, sure.

It's just . . .

I have to see a therapist once a week and I have to talk about my life and about my problems, but I won't take the pills anymore. I took them for a while, but I don't like them and so I stopped taking them. They take away the lows but they take away the highs, too, and so you're left floating in a strange in-between of colorless, tasteless moments.

And it's not like . . .

I don't want to kill myself.

It's just that sometimes I can't understand anything, and sometimes it feels like the whole weight of the universe settles itself on my shoulders and I can't see the reason for anything. I don't want to die, really, but I don't particularly want to live.

Sometimes I wish I could slip away while I sleep. Wake up someplace better. Someplace quieter.

But I don't believe in heaven, so I'm not sure where that place would be.

I made the mistake of telling people this. So I was sent to a psychiatrist.

And it's gotten better since then.

I don't know.

Sometimes it's fine. Sometimes I'm fine.

Other days.

It's hard for me to have a conversation. It's hard for me to get up, brush my teeth, comb my hair.

It's hard for me to face my friends at school. It's hard for me to write a research paper. It's hard for me to take a breath. Air, sometimes, seems too thick. Tastes like smoke.

I don't know why I feel that way. I have a great life. It's perfect, really. My parents are fine. My brother is fine. My sister is fine. My friends are fine. Things are fine.

This is what I keep telling my therapist, but he keeps making me go back and back and back.

He says, Do you sometimes get the feeling you'll never be happy?

I say, Don't we all?

He writes something down on a little pad of paper.

I say, I was just . . . That was a joke. I was joking.

He says, Do you always joke like that?

I say, Oh god, Alex.

He lets me call him Alex.

I haven't told him about my missing time.

Like I said, I haven't told anyone.

I kind of want to . . .

Just figure it out. See if I can figure it out by myself.

I just hate thinking there's a part of myself I don't understand. That I can't control, that I can't tame, that I can't stop. That I can't change. It makes me crazy. It makes me angry. It makes me scared. It's scary.

One minute you're in history class and it's ten thirty in the morning, and the next minute you're driving your car and you can't find your cell phone and you don't know what time it is and how many hours you've lost and where you've been and what you did and whether you haven't just lost your entire fucking mind.

That's what it feels like. Like I've lost my entire fucking mind. Like I've gone crazy and like I'll never be normal and like I should just pack my things the second I turn eighteen, move to Alaska or Scotland or Romania. Get as far away as I can from everyone I love and just lead my life in a quiet town, knitting sweaters and selling them on street corners to pay my rent and buy food.

I can't knit. I would learn.

I look at myself in the rearview window. I look the same as I looked this morning. I have my hair in a bun and I look tired. I'm on Water Street, I'm driving through the touristy section of town; there are small shops on either side of me. My parents own a shop here. Was I coming to see them? There it is, on the right. By-the-Sea Books. I work there after school some days. They only pay me minimum wage. I know for a fact the other cashiers get more. My parents say yes, but the other cashiers do not get dinner and a place to live and clothes to wear and a car to drive.

Fair enough.

I put my signal on and take a left onto Prince Street.

Should I go back to school? Make up some excuse about where I've been? Sick grandmother? I use that excuse a lot. My grandmother is dead. All my grandparents are dead. No one knows that. You say sick grandmother and people don't usually ask questions.

Right on Allen Street.

I'll go back home, take a shower, take a nap. Be back at the bookstore by five and hope they don't call my mom before then. Tell her I skipped out again. Maybe they'll call my dad. He's a lot easier to deal with. He gets flustered and takes any excuse I give him with a hint of gratefulness. He just wants to believe I'm not crazy.

I don't want to go back to school. It's hard to get back into the sway of everything after you've been outside yourself for a few hours. Or inside yourself. Or next to yourself. Somewhere else. Who knows?

Left on Prescott.

That's when I see him.

There's more traffic on Prescott. It leads into the center of town and it spans the length of Manchester. Quickest way through.

I see him from far off in my rearview mirror. I don't know what makes me see him. The motorcyclist. He's dressed in black. Black jacket, black helmet. He's going too fast. He's weaving in and out of traffic and I know something awful is going to happen before it happens. I feel like I've seen him before, the boy on the motorcycle, and I feel like I know it's inevitable, what's about to happen. He's speeding through cars, he's riding the yellow line, he's gaining on me, and I know it's me he's coming for. It's me, I'm the reason he's speeding. He's trying to catch up to me.

But that's crazy.

I look up as the light turns yellow, but I'm already

halfway through the intersection so I keep going.

The boy on the bike, he's not slowing down. The cars around him are stopping for the red light, but he's speeding up and he's trying to beat the traffic that's already crossing Prescott on Jacobson.

For a second I think he's going to make it.

But then he doesn't.

The truck hits his back tire and he's in the air and I'm screaming without realizing it, braking without meaning to, and I lose him somewhere over the roof of my car. The squealing of tires and the crash as a second car hits the truck that hit his bike and suddenly the boy has landed on the road in front of me. He's flown off his bike and clear through the air over my car, and I don't know how I've gotten out of my car but I'm out and I'm still screaming and I'm running over to him like, I don't know. Like I can save him. But there's blood on the pavement and there's blood leaking out of his helmet and his leg, one of his legs—it's broken, it's bent all wrong. And I know he's going to die. I don't know how I know but I know, and I fall to the pavement in front of him and I pull his helmet off. Because why? Because I don't know. It's all I can do.

His eyes are open. He's gasping for breath. His eyes are green, his hair is black, his lips are red with blood that's choking up out of his mouth.

Fuck, fuck, fuck, fuck, I say and I pick his head off the pavement and cradle it in the crook of my elbow and there's blood all over my sweater. My favorite sweater and there's blood all over it.

Fuck, I say. Please don't die. I can't watch you die.

He catches his breath a little. I wipe the blood away from his mouth with my spare sleeve and I'm crying suddenly; I didn't realize I was crying. This stranger is going to die and I don't want him to die. Please don't die. Please don't die.

His eyes focus on my face. His eyes meet mine and run over my mouth, my neck, my ears, my hair. Back to my face, my eyes.

"Mabel," he says.

Mabel?

"I'm not . . . Look, it's okay, you're not going to die."

"Molly," he says.

He said Molly?

He said my name?

How do you? How do you . . . How do you? How do you?

"How do you know my name?" I whisper.

"I fucked up," he says.

"How do you know my name?"

"It's me," he says. "It's Lyle."

"I don't . . ."

I don't know you.

"Please don't leave me."

"I'm not going to leave you."

"I fucked up again. I always fuck it up. I just. I wanted to see you again. I couldn't . . . I had to try."

"I don't know who you are."

"You can't leave me," he says. "You have to stay with me until I die."

"You're not . . . Don't say that. You're not going to die."

You can't die in front of me.

"I'm going to die," he says, "of course I'm going to die. I feel like I'm going to die."

"You're . . . you're not making any sense."

"You were starting to . . . Molly, please. Don't leave me."

"How do you know my name?"

He's choking again; fresh blood is bubbling out of his mouth and all I can see is the red of it spreading out in one big puddle on the pavement. His eyes are rolling backward in his head, and suddenly I'm aware there are people standing around us. People screaming, a woman crying. He's going to die.

"Lyle!" I yell. I shake him. "Lyle! Wake up!"

His eyes flutter open again; I wipe the blood from his mouth.

"Don't die, please," I beg.

"Get in the ambulance," he says and then I can hear it, the ambulance, the sirens. "Ride in the ambulance with me. Tell them you know me. My name is Lyle Avery. My cell phone is in my pocket. Call my brother. Tell him . . .

tell him where to meet us."

"I don't know how you know me," I say. I choke. "I don't know who you are."

"I know," he says, "but I had to try."

The sirens are getting closer. The ring of people around us is growing, but nobody tries to help. "Please don't die," I whisper.

"You have to call my brother. In my phone. His name is Sayer."

Sayer Avery.

"I don't know who you are," I say weakly.

"At least pretend," he says. "I need you to pretend."

The woman sobs louder. Lyle coughs again, and blood sprays from his lips and gets all over me.

He's going to die. He's going to die and there's nothing I can do.

In the times I'd like to black out, I am forced to live. To be aware. To witness.

In the times I'd like to wake up hours away from where I am, miles away from where I am, I am here. Here watching this boy I do not know take ragged, choking breaths. His teeth stained red. His eyes all white. His cheeks draining of color.

"Lyle," I say, and he focuses on my face again. "Lyle. You're going to be okay."

I love you and you're not going to die.

TWO.

Someone pulls me away from him.

The EMTs are here; they're strapping him to a stretcher. One of them asks me his name and they yell it at him, trying to get him to open his eyes. I step forward without thinking and reach into his pocket, find his phone, and pull it out. Somebody grabs me, holds my arms, looks into my face as if scared I might be hurt, too.

No, no. It's all his blood. I'm okay, I'm fine. I'm fine.

Then they're loading the stretcher into the ambulance and I'm stumbling forward, screaming suddenly, mad with fear that they'll take him from me, that he'll die without me.

"Lyle!" I scream. "Please, I have to go with him! Please!"

"You know him?" one of the EMTs says. A skinny boy with red hair. He's too young to be an EMT—how can he save anyone's life?

"He's my friend, please. I have to go with him; I have to be with him. He's my friend. He's Lyle Avery. His name is Lyle Avery."

He doesn't want to let me come. I can tell by the split-second shadow that crosses his face. But he makes up his mind and he grabs my arm and he pushes me up into the back of the ambulance and he shuts the doors behind me and I make myself as small as I can as these people try to save Lyle's life.

They put an oxygen mask over his face, but he pulls it off and he says, "Molly? Molly?"

"I'm here. Lyle, I'm here," I say, and I move to put a hand on his jeans but there's blood all over everything and his leg is broken and so instead I pull my hand away and put it on my lap and then . . .

And then, nothing.

We're at the hospital. I'm standing in a hallway and I'm holding Lyle's cell phone in my hand and the last ten, fifteen minutes, they're gone. I don't remember them. I'm covered in blood and people are staring at me as they walk by and I'm looking at a pair of closed double doors and I know Lyle is somewhere behind those doors, dying.

My hands are covered in blood. I scroll through the list of contacts in Lyle's phone and I find him, Sayer, the brother. And I press the button to call and I hold the phone up to my ear and I realize my hands are shaking. And I'm still crying, somehow, and my head is pounding and I take steps backward until I hit the wall because without it I'm going to pass out. My legs are going to give way.

I don't answer him when he says hello.

I try to, but when I open my mouth, I start crying harder, and then he says my name and I drop the phone on the floor and I slide down the wall and put my face in my hands and cry.

I want to know this boy, but he's going to die, and I want to know where I go when I black out and I want to know why I feel so sad all the time and why I want to go to sleep and never wake up. And then someone else has picked the phone up off the floor and they tell Sayer where to go. They whisper to hurry, they tell him his friend's really upset and he should get here as soon as he can.

And then nothing again. I wake up and I'm in a quiet, private waiting room and there's a boy sitting across from me who could be Lyle's twin, only he's older and he's not bleeding and he's not dying and he's not dead.

"Hey," he says.

"When did you get here?" I say.

"Twenty minutes ago. They gave you something to calm you down. You might be a little groggy."

It's the perfect excuse. I don't have to pretend to remember anything.

"You're Sayer."

He nods. He has the same green eyes and dark hair as his brother.

"I don't know who you are," I say.

"I know."

"I don't know how you know me."

"I don't know you."

"You said my name on the phone. How did you know my name?"

"The medication," he says. "What they gave you. Everything might be a little fuzzy."

"But you said my name," I say. "On the phone, when you answered, you said my name."

"No," he says sadly, shaking his head. "I don't know your name. I don't know how you know my brother."

"I just . . . I saw the accident. He asked me to call you."

"Thank you," he says. "I really appreciate that."

"I'm Molly," I say. My head is pounding. It feels like I've made all of it up, that none of it happened. Of course he doesn't know me. Of course he never said my name on the phone. How would he know my name? "Is your brother okay?"

"He's going to die," he answers me. His face is sad but even. He doesn't cry.

"Did they tell you that?"

"They didn't have to tell me," he says.

"But there has to be some . . ."

"Of course," he says.

And then we're quiet. There is this enormous emptiness in between us and it is filled with my head pounding and with the dried blood on my hands and on my sweater, and it is filled with Sayer's quiet breathing and the way he looks at his knees. And it's like I'm pulled to him. I get up and I stumble and I almost fall, but he's risen and he's caught me by the elbows and there's nothing except Sayer and this waiting room. The way he pulls me closer to him and the way he rocks me back and forth. The smell of blood and the sting of tears and the heavy fog of the medicine they gave me.

And then the door opens and the doctor comes in. The doctor's covered in blood, too, and he stands there, shaking his head. He still has his gloves on. He realizes it and he pulls them off and he holds them in a ball in his hands. They are blue. I try not to look at them.

Sayer pulls away from me, but he holds my hand.

And the doctor says, "I'm sorry we couldn't save him. We did everything we could but we still couldn't save him."

He says more. He's talking to Sayer but I don't hear any of it. And I feel myself slipping away again, but it's in slow motion and I know I don't have to go. I can stay here. I need to stay here. It's late. I need to call my parents. I left my car in the middle of the street with the engine running, and I left my phone and my purse in the car, and I left school early, and I have no idea what's going on. Everything normal and ordinary is slipping away from me and the dead boy knew my name. Lyle, he's dead. He knew me, somehow, and now he's dead.

I let go of Sayer's hand and I sit down in a chair, and the doctor is still talking but I can't hear what he says. It's like my ears are clogged. It's like no matter how hard I try to hear him, his voice is a blur. Like he's talking to me, but I'm in a swimming pool and his words hit the water and the sound waves split up and turn warped and wobbly.

And then he's gone. Sayer sits down across from me again, and I realize he has Lyle's phone in his hands now and he's twirling it around and around. So I hold my hand out without saying anything, and he gives it to me and the clock on the front of it says seven.

I dial my mother's number and she answers, yelling and worried, and then when I ask her to pick me up at the hospital, she stops yelling and her voice gets so soft I can barely make out her half-formed questions. "Okay? Jesus, what? Hospital? What are you . . . Molly? Molly, what's happened?"

"I'm fine, please," I say. "Please just come and get me."

I hang up the phone and put it on the chair next to me. I look up at Sayer. His hands are shaking. He's holding them in a tight ball on his lap and they're shaking.

I can't stay here anymore. I can't stay in this room with

him anymore. I stand up and he reaches toward me and touches my wrist.

"Where are you going?" he says.

"I'm going home," I say. "I'm sorry about your brother."

"You don't have to go."

"I do," I say, "I really do. I have to go. I'm sorry."

"Can I . . ."

"No, please."

I don't know what he wants, but I know I can't do it.

I'm out of the waiting room and I'm practically running down the hallway and out the door, and when the air hits me, I inhale deeply and I sit down on the curb and put my head between my knees and I feel the rush of nausea like I've been expecting it. But I will not throw up. Not now, here. I won't throw up. I will wait until I am alone and clean and then I will brush my teeth and tomorrow I will get up and go to school and I will see my friends and this will be like a bad dream. Like a nightmare. Like something unfortunate that happened but is now over. And the boy on the motorcycle knew my name, sure, but stranger things have happened. Stranger things have happened to me.

THREE.

My mom and my dad come to get me in the mini-van and they both jump out as soon as it stops and my mom is crying and my dad looks terrified—he looks white and he looks like he's about to fall over—and I'm trying to explain to them that I'm fine, that none of this is my blood and I'm fine, I'm just hungry and I'm just tired and we should go and find my car and then go home, can we please go home? In the van my mom makes my dad drive and she sits in the back with me and hugs me close to her, and at some point I mention that this was my favorite sweater and I make her laugh a little, which is a relief. And my car, it's fine, someone has moved it to the side of the road and left my keys underneath the seat. My mom won't let me drive and so she follows us and it's just my dad and me in the minivan. The minivan smells like books because on the weekends my parents take long drives to thrift stores and they buy the books they'll resell in the bookstore. I've always loved the smell of this mini-van. It's mold, I know, but it's comforting.

"You're sure you're okay, Molly?" my dad says.

"Not okay," I say. "Freaked out. But I'll live."

"You did a very honorable thing."

I explained it to them on the way to get my car. The short version. I saw the accident, I held the dying boy. He died.

"I'm not going to tell your mother," he says.

"About what?"

"The school called me. You skipped most of your classes today."

He doesn't seem angry. The upside of watching some-one die. You get away with more, at least temporarily.

"God, yeah. Stupid. I'm . . . I'm sorry. I'm really sorry."

I couldn't help it. I don't remember anything.

"We count on you, Molly. To set a good example."

"Dad, I can't . . . can we just . . ."

"Not another word." He puts his hand on my leg and squeezes. "I was so scared when I saw you outside the hos-pital. You looked . . ."

"Like I was the one who was hit by a car?"

"Yeah," he says, shaking his head. "You didn't know the boy, you said?"

"No. I've never seen him before."

"It's such a shame. I've always said motorcycles—"

"Coffins on wheels, I know."

"I'll stop," he says. "I'm just . . ."

"I know."

At home Hazel and Clancy are sitting at the kitchen table and they don't say anything when we walk in the front door. My mother, she must have called them and warned them. Don't say anything. Your sister is fine; just don't say anything. She says she'll warm me up some leftovers and I excuse myself to take a shower. In the bathroom I throw up three times, but it's only acid and water. I haven't eaten all day. Or maybe I have—I can't remember.

I feel better after the shower and after dinner, even though the four of them sit there and watch me eat and Hazel keeps jumping up to get me water and even Clancy is quiet and keeps looking at me when he thinks I won't catch him looking at me. I make eye contact with him once but turn away quickly. Everyone says I look exactly like Clancy. After dinner I excuse myself and I brush my teeth and when I go into my room Hazel is sitting cross-legged on my bed.

Clancy and I have brown hair and brown eyes, but Hazel's eyes are blue and her hair is blond and she keeps it short and pixielike. We tell her she's adopted because she doesn't even look like our parents or the photos we have of our grandparents. She doesn't look like anyone, but there are pictures of our mother pregnant. Our mother's showed us, as proof. "Stop bugging your sister," she said once, pulling a photo from a shoe box and sliding it across the table at us.

"This could be anyone," Clancy had said, pointing at her bulging stomach.

"I'm tired, Hazel," I say now, and then I see Clancy at the window seat. He's staring out the window like he doesn't really want to be here. Clancy's like me in personality as well as appearance. He prefers being by himself. "Is this an intervention?" I ask him.

"Not my idea," he says quickly.

"I'm fine, Hazel. I'm tired," I insist.

"It's important to talk about things, Molly," Hazel says.

Thirteen years old and she thinks it's important to talk about things.

"She doesn't want to talk," Clancy says quickly.

"It's important," Hazel repeats.

"Can she talk to you, then? She might want to talk to you," he says.

"I don't actually want to talk to either of you," I say. "No offense, Hazel. I'm fine; I'm tired."

"Well," she says, jumping off the bed, "I'll be in my room if you need me." She slips quietly out of the room.

Clancy hasn't moved from the window seat.

"Must have been crazy," he says.

"Sure," I say. "Crazy."

"You actually saw him—"

"Clancy."

"Right, sorry."

He stands up awkwardly, uncomfortable in his own skin, something I could always relate to. Clancy isn't in therapy, though. He's never admitted to anyone that he sometimes might rather be dead.

"Good night," I say.

"Hey, don't off yourself tonight," he says, brightening. Depression humor. He shuts the door when he leaves.

In my dreams I see his face.

Bloody and white on the pavement. The blood warm and filling his mouth, spilling over and pooling underneath him. The white of his eyeballs.

I see both their faces; they are interchangeable. The brothers, Lyle and Sayer. Lyle Avery. Dead now.

What had he said?

He wanted to see me again.

My dreams twist his face into a demon, into an angel, into a red mass of unrecognizable flesh. I wake up sweaty and panicked twenty times until finally I get out of bed. It's five in the morning and I go downstairs to make myself a cup of coffee.

It's Wednesday. I get my backpack from the living room. Someone brought it in for me last night. I have homework and I work on it at the kitchen table until my mom comes down and offers breakfast. Scrambled eggs? Toast? I'm not hungry, but I eat whatever she puts in front of me because it's easier than arguing. My brother stumbles down around six; and Hazel, dressed and bright and cheerful, bounces into the kitchen at seven thirty. And if I thought my parents might give me the option to stay home, they don't. My mother kisses my cheek and my dad gives me one of his long, meaningful shoulder squeezes and then they practically herd us outside.

I drop Hazel off at middle school and then Clancy and I make our way to the high school. We never talk in the mornings. He's brought coffee in a travel mug, but he gives it to me. This is his way of making sure I'm okay. Have some coffee; don't be sad. He'd never be able to actually say it.

Erie and Luka are by my locker, waiting. They don't know about the accident, but they know I left school early yesterday and they want an explanation. Erie is indignant and offended I didn't ask her to bail with me.

"Didn't return any of my text messages," Erie says, in lieu of *hello*. I realize I haven't looked at my phone for a long time. I didn't even get it out of my backpack this morning. I fish around for it now and withdraw it triumphantly: dead. I show it to her.

"Dead," I say, shrugging.

"And your charger is, what, lost?" she insists. Erie is holding her phone and showing it to me like this is what a phone is supposed to look like, Molly. Fully charged.

"Maybe lost," I say. I haven't actually seen it in a while.

"You're impossible," she says.

"You missed a test," Luka says.

"What subject?" I ask. But I don't really care. I shove past him to get to my locker and open it quickly, withdrawing unneeded books from my bag and stacking them inside.

"Health," he says.

"Tragic," I say. Health isn't a class; it's a subset of gym. Nobody's ever failed gym.

"It was pretty important," he persists. He has a book in his hands; he uses it to gesture and it slips out of his fingers and lands on Erie's toe. It's a hardcover; her reaction is elaborate and loud.

"I don't care about the fucking test, Luka," I moan, slamming my locker shut and resting my head for a moment against its metal surface.

"Well, you shouldn't be wearing sandals in October," Luka is saying. He straightens up and puts the book into his backpack. Erie holds one foot off the ground and whimpers.

"They're the only shoes I have that go with this shirt," she says, pouting.

"Do they really go with that shirt, though?" Luka asks.

"How would you even know what goes with this shirt?" Erie shoots back.

"Can I have some quiet time? I'm imposing quiet time," I interject.

"What's wrong with you?" Luka asks.

And Erie says, "Luka just dropped a *book* on my foot and you're the one who needs special treatment?"

"Your foot is fine," Luka says.

"Really. Guys. Really," I say.

They leave me alone. Erie shoots me a bewildered look and Luka shoots me a tired, patronizing look; and then they talk to each other and they let me be quiet and we walk together through the hallways, but it's really the two of them and then me. Separate.

I just . . . sometimes I can't talk to people. And they've known me for a long time; they get it.

It's good to have friends like this because you don't have to explain things to them right away. Eventually I'll have to tell them about the accident and about dead Lyle Avery, but for now we're just walking to class. And sometimes they say my name to involve me in the conversation and I nod like I'm listening but I'm not expected to respond. I'm not expected to do anything other than just walk beside them.

Before lunch Erie can't wait anymore and she corners me outside the cafeteria.

"You haven't said a word to me all day," she says.

"That is an exaggeration," I say.

Erie sometimes thinks everything in the world is happening to her or against her or because of her. She considers herself to be a very involved participant in the lives of her friends.

"What, are you like—are you *okay*? You know? Are you?"

She says *okay* in a way that really means—*Are you having a bad day?* Like, *Are you feeling more depressed than usual?* Like, *Should I call someone and tell them?*

You make one comment about maybe wanting to die and this is how your friends will treat you forever and ever, like you are a loaded gun in the hands of someone incredibly jumpy.

"I had a rough night. I'm fine. I'll tell you later."

Erie shakes her head; her long California blond hair gives off a light of its own, that's how shiny it is. She makes her way to our usual spot in the cafeteria, a table in the back by the window. She sits down with her new weird poet boyfriend, Carbon, who sometimes goes through these phases where he only speaks in rhyme.

I don't know if that's really his name.

I get in line and pick out my usual grilled cheese sandwich, apple, coffee. My school starting serving coffee after a month-long struggle involving mostly Clancy and me passing petitions around during study halls. We threatened a sit-in and they eventually provided us with these packets of instant coffee and hot water.

In front of me in line is Bret Jennings. I try and make myself as unnoticeable as possible, because the last time I saw Bret, I spilled the majority of my orange juice on his sneakers.

"Hey, Molly," he says.

So much for unnoticeable.

"Oh, hey. How are you?"

"Drier than the last time you saw me."

Oh, jokes. He has jokes.

"Have I mentioned how completely sorry I am for the orange juice incident?"

"A couple times," he says, and smiles.

"I, um, well . . . well, we both have apples. For lunch."

We both have apples?

"Astute, Molly," he says, but he's still smiling.

"It's, um, your turn. To pay."

He turns away from me. We both have apples. I could die now, really. In this lunch line.

"Well, see you," he says after he's given the lunch lady his money.

I pay for my food and try and get to my table without making eye contact with anyone else. Luka has saved a seat for me between him and Erie, but Erie's talking to Carbon anyway and, besides, I can't tell them *now*, with all these extra people around. So I lean in to Erie and promise I'll come over after my appointment. That's what we call my meetings with Alex. It's every Wednesday after school and we refer to it as my appointment so it could be any number of other, cooler things. An appointment to do illegal drugs with interesting people. An appointment to continue my studies in assassin techniques and strategies. Luka and Erie are the only ones who know what it really is.

I drink my coffee and wait for the inevitable visit from Clancy, who generally takes it upon himself to relieve me of my leftover lunch money in order to buy himself seconds of everything. Not long after he's gone, the bell rings and I realize I have study hall next and I never did the English reading. I've forgotten the textbook somewhere in the backseat of my car, so I excuse myself from Luka and Erie and of course it's drizzling outside now, out of nowhere, so I'm going to get soaked.

I don't have an umbrella and I don't have time to get my coat from my locker so I have nothing to put over my head and as a result I get rain all in my hair and my face and my eyes and so everything is a little blurry and it takes me a minute before I see him, leaning against my car underneath a huge umbrella. I rub rain out of my eyes with the back of my hand, realizing too late that I've effectively smeared mascara all over my face.

It's Sayer Avery. He looks like he's waiting for me, but he also looks like he was hoping I'd never come and now that I'm here he's a little disappointed.

"Hey, um . . . What are you doing here?" I say.

He lifts the umbrella higher, steps away from the car, offers it to me.

I duck under it without thinking. There's plenty of room for both of us. It's an enormous umbrella. A golf umbrella. Like a tarp on a stick.

I'm really glad I didn't say any of that out loud.

"Hi, Molly," he says.

"What are you doing here?" I repeat.

"I wanted to . . . thank you again. For everything you did for my brother. They told me you stayed with him. They told me no one else would go near him, but you stayed with him." He seems genuine and I'm about to respond when I think—how did he find my car? There's only one high school in Manchester, sure, but my car? He was leaning against my car. Not anybody else's. I look at my car and then I look at him.

"How did you know this is my car?"

"They gave me a description. The EMTs. I wanted to find you," he says without hesitation.

"And you just thought you'd . . . wait for me? In the rain? Until I showed up?"

His face changes. For a minute he is lost, confused, sad. Here he is, his brother just died and I'm treating him to a game of twenty questions.

"I'm sorry," I say quickly, backpedaling. "I don't know why I can be so . . . Look, I'm just sorry. About everything.

About your brother."

"I shouldn't have shown up. It must look a little weird."

"It doesn't look weird at all. Really, I'm . . . It doesn't look weird."

He fidgets with something on the umbrella handle. It's the little loop you can put around your wrist. He twists it around one finger. He twists it and untwists it. He looks like he wants to say something. He looks like he's trying to find words that haven't been invented yet. And I don't know why but I want to be close to him. It's like I didn't even know he existed until yesterday but now that I do, I just want him to never leave again. I want to stay here in this parking lot with him forever. I want to freeze time. I want this rain, this umbrella, this moment—forever.

"The funeral is Saturday," he says after a long pause.

"Oh," I say.

"I'd like you to go. I mean . . . I came here to see if you could go."

"Oh," I say again. "Sure."

"We don't know a lot of people here. My parents are dead. Not a lot of family left. I just . . . I don't know, I thought it would be nice if you could come."

"I'm . . . Of course, Sayer. Of course I'll go."

"Can I have your number?" he says, taking his phone from his pocket. "I'll text you the information."

"Oh, sure," I say. I give him my number. I'll charge my phone tonight.

"See you, Molly," he says.

And he's gone. Just like that.

And I don't want him to go but I can't ask him to stay. I don't even know him.

FOUR.

After school I drop Hazel and Clancy off at the bookstore and head over to Alex's office. It's in the middle of town and I have to drive down Prescott Street again and every time I look in the rearview mirror I see Lyle's bike speeding toward me, weaving in and out of traffic. The truck hitting his back tire. His body flying over the roof of my car. His body hitting the pavement. His body breaking and bleeding.

The man with the two o'clock appointment is older and he always comes out at five of three exactly, crying and red-faced and avoiding all eye contact. That's fine by me. I can avoid eye contact with the best of them.

Sometimes I wonder what Alex does in those five minutes between this man's appointment and my appointment, but it's probably something uninteresting. He probably arranges his notes. Sharpens the pencils that are on his desk. Makes sure his books are still alphabetized.

I like Alex, really. He's in his late thirties, maybe, and he's attractive and he's only rarely prying. Usually he lets me do the talking, and if I don't feel like talking sometimes we play cards or I let him read a short story I'm working on. He asks me if I want to be a writer, but I've never really thought much about it. I like books, of course; I was practically raised on them. The bookstore is older than I am. There's a room in the back where my parents kept a crib.

"Hello, Molly."

"Hey, Alex."

I'm ushered into his tiny office, all bookshelves and hardcover copies of weird psychology encyclopedias. He's pulled the shades half shut for me; too much light bothers my eyes.

"And how are we this week?" he says.

I collapse in the armchair gratefully, letting my body sink into the cushions.

"I saw somebody die," I say. No use beating around the bush.

He's reaching for his reading glasses. His hand pauses and his eyes dart to my face, checking if I'm lying. He doesn't put it past me. Sometimes I say things just for his reaction and then I laugh like a maniac while he shakes his head and explains to me that all jokes stem from some sort of real feeling and would I like to maybe talk about that in more depth?

"You're serious?"

"Prescott and Jacobson," I say. "Motorcycle accident."

"That was . . . I saw that on the news this morning," he says. He hasn't picked up his notebook yet. I told him once I hate when he writes while I talk. It's distracting.

"He flew over my car," I say. "He landed on the pavement in front of me. I had to slam on my brakes. I could have run over him. I mean—I almost did. I almost ran over him."

"Molly, that's awful. I'm so sorry you had to see that," he says. He's sincere. But there's something else. I don't know what it is. It's like he's searching my face for someone else.

"It wasn't my fault. The truck behind me hit him. The truck behind me hit his tire."

"Of course," Alex says. "It was an accident. It wasn't your fault."

"There's more," I say, and I wait for him to gesture: continue. "I got out of the car. I wanted to see if he was okay."

"And?"

"I took off his helmet. And . . . there was blood everywhere. There was a lot of blood."

Suddenly it's hard to talk about. Suddenly I can only see Lyle's face and Lyle's eyes looking into mine. He looked so sad, but he looked so happy to have reached me.

"Take your time," Alex says.

I take a deep breath. "Something weird happened."

"What was that?"

"He . . ." I don't know why I'm telling him this. Usually I don't tell him things like this. He always tells me to be honest with him and my parents always tell me to be honest with him but I always leave things out because I don't want to go back on the medication, because I don't want him to send me away. Because I don't want to end up in an insane asylum. They still have them. They still exist. "He knew my name, Alex. He kept saying that he knew me, and that he wanted to catch up to me. Like he . . . wanted to see me or something. He said he fucked up again. That's what he said. And then I told him he was going to be okay and he said he knew he was going to die."

Alex leans back a little in his chair. His eyes are big and sympathetic. "Molly, a person can say some pretty confusing things when he's that hurt. His brain isn't working properly; his body is expending all its energy on healing its wounds. He doesn't have time for much cognitive activity."

"He knew my name, Alex. He said my name."

"This is a small town, Molly."

"No, this was different. He acted like he knew me. Like he *really* knew me. But I'd never seen him before."

"Friend of a friend? Someone you met one time and never thought about again?"

Was it possible? I search back through a year of disjointed memories. All the blank spots, the missing time, keep jumping to the surface. I know I've never seen his face before. I would have remembered him.

Or . . .

I don't know.

Maybe I wouldn't have.

Maybe I don't.

"I don't think so," I say, but now I'm not so sure.

"Nobody wants to experience something like that by themselves. Even if he'd only met you once, Molly, enough to know your name, he might have invented a stronger connection with you, to help himself."

This makes sense.

This makes sense, doesn't it?

"Do you think that's possible?"

"Of course. Think about it. If you were so injured you thought you might not make it, wouldn't you want to be with someone—anyone? As opposed to a perfect stranger? Or by yourself?"

It's a far better explanation than any I've been able to come up with.

"Tell me what else," he continues. "What happened after the accident?"

"He asked me to ride with him in the ambulance and

he told me to call his brother for him. I took his cell phone and then in the hospital we were in a private waiting room and it felt weird. The brother and me. It felt like I was intruding on something."

"You didn't feel like you had a right to share his grief."

"I was covered in blood, Alex," I continue. "The brother, he, um . . . he asked me to go to the funeral. On Saturday."

"Are you going to go?"

"Do you think I should?"

"I think it might bring you a sense of closure. He probably invited you because you were there for his brother when no one else was. There is nothing wrong with declining his invitation, but I think it might be a good experience."

Since when did I let any experience be good.

I don't say that out loud.

What I do say is, "Thanks, Alex. It was, um . . . really helpful. To talk to you."

"I think that's the first time you've ever thanked me, Molly."

And I don't blame him for looking just the smallest bit pleased with himself.

When I finally get home and plug my phone into the wall, it's been dead for over twenty-four hours and I have approximately thirty-seven text messages from Erie, the last one received about a half hour ago, asking me if

I think it will be easy to find a new fucking best friend who's prepared to put up with all my dead-phone bullshit. I text her back and tell her to come over after dinner. She responds immediately—*OK*.

Nothing from Sayer yet.

And nothing from Luka, but that's no surprise. He's worse with his phone than I am.

At dinner my family is back to their regular selves. So I've discovered how long dead-boy sympathy lasts around here and it's less than one full day. Although I shouldn't say that. Mom has brought my favorite dessert home—lemon meringue pie—and Dad pours me a small glass of wine without even asking. Clancy is his usual brooding self, pushing his peas around on his plate like he's trying to figure out what they're saying to him, and Hazel chirps tirelessly on about her perfect day, her perfect friends, her perfect life.

Fucking alien.

The doorbell rings halfway through dessert but Erie lets herself in without bothering to wait for any of us. She eats an entire second dinner at an impressive pace and consumes two pieces of pie in less than six minutes. She has the metabolism of—I don't know—a hummingbird. Something that eats a lot and moves like a blur and somehow stays annoyingly skinny.

I'm not as skinny as her. I have a fuller face and a small waist but bigger thighs and hips.

I'm not looking forward to retelling everything to Erie, but I've already decided I'll leave out all the weird stuff. The more I think about Alex's take on things, the more I realize how unnecessarily freaked I've been. Especially with Erie, who finds a way to blow the simplest situation amazingly out of proportion. I'll stick to the basics. Dead boy. Ambulance. Brother. Funeral. The end.

I should call Luka, I know, and tell them both together, but the idea of the two of them is exhausting. I'm tired. I'm always tired on Wednesdays and I still have homework to do and it's already seven. I was supposed to wash my hair tonight. I still could—maybe Erie will braid it for me.

Erie's my oldest friend. She moved from California to Massachusetts when she was five and her mom walked into my parents' bookstore and asked for a job. She rang as a cashier for a little while until she found something more permanent and that's how I met Erie. She was always hanging around in the children's section, pulling endless books off the shelf to see whether they had enough pictures. At five years old I was reshelving her discards. Not much has changed.

Her full name is Erie Black, no middle name. Or, that's what I'm supposed to tell people. Really, her full name is Erie Moon Black, but I'm not allowed to ever repeat that, ever, under penalty of her revealing that I once peed in the middle of the hallway in my sleep. When I was fourteen.

We all have secrets.

After dinner Erie and I head up to my room and she plops herself down on her stomach on my bed and I take the window seat and she doesn't take her cell phone out, which from her is a sign of utmost respect. She realizes I have something important to tell her.

So I tell her.

I leave out the weird parts—the lost time (of course) and Lyle knowing my name and Sayer meeting me by my car. I do tell her he asked me to the funeral but I omit the details.

When I'm done, Erie has shifted to sitting cross-legged, her face in her hands and her blue eyes wide and alert. You have to work for it sometimes, but Erie can be the best kind of listener. She never says anything until you're done, and she's completely riveted if it's a good enough story.

"Wow," she breathes when it's clear I've told her everything. "Wow, Molly, that's just . . . I can't believe it. Are you going?"

"Alex thinks it's a good idea."

It helps to call him Alex. You could just be talking about one of your other friends. Not your head doctor.

"If you want me to go with you . . ."

"I don't think Sayer would want me to bring anyone. He said it's going to be small."

"Let me know," she says. Her face has changed a little. Slightly. Like she was about to say something and then remembered she couldn't. "Sayer, huh? That's a weird name."

I shrug. "He seems nice."

"But they're not from around here?" she says. "We would have met them before."

It's true. The towns are so small around here that we even know people from two and three high schools over.

"Could be new," I say.

"This is awful, Molly," she says, and she actually shudders. "That you had to see all that. Had to go to the hospital, even. Your fault for skipping school and not inviting me."

"I didn't plan on it," I say.

"You left five minutes before the bell rang. Couldn't you have waited?"

"I did?" I say, and then I nod my head vigorously, realizing that I'm supposed to know this. "Obviously, sure, I did."

"Who texted you, anyway?"

"What?"

"You got a message on your phone. I saw you read it. And then you wrote something back and you just got up and left."

This was interesting. I'd never pressed my friends for information about how I acted when I lost time. When I tried it on Hazel, she saw through me in a second. I'm apparently not very good at pretending to be normal.

I don't remember getting a text message.

"Unrelated," I say unconvincingly. What else am I supposed to say? Was it related? I have absolutely no idea.

Erie raises her eyebrows. "Doubt it," she says.

"Suit yourself."

"Let me see your phone, then."

Should I? Not like I can really stop her from just grabbing it, anyway; it's on the desk and she's faster than me. Besides, maybe I'll find out something interesting. I nod my chin at it. She reaches and picks it up before I can change my mind, and starts scrolling eagerly through my messages. Erie respects privacy as much as my parents respect an offhanded joke about suicide. Which is to say, you know, not at all.

Then, crestfallen, she says, "You deleted it! Not fair, Molly!"

I go with my safest response: a shrug.

"There's nothing here from yesterday morning," she continues. "You're tricky. Who are you talking to that you don't want me to know about?"

"Your boyfriend, maybe."

She throws a pillow at me. I catch it and hug it to my stomach. I feel weird. What did Erie see? Who sent me a message? Why had it made me leave?

"Oh, incoming," she says suddenly, twisting my phone around so I can see the screen.

"Who is it? Luka? I was supposed to call him."

"Private," she says.

Private? Who do I know that's private?

"Oh," she continues. That weird expression again. Made

weirder because generally if Erie wants to say something, she'll say it. "Funeral details." She tosses me the phone.

I feel a weird chill as I realize she's right. It's the address and the time of the funeral Saturday. But the number's private. How am I supposed to text him back, let him know if I can go or not?

Then another text:

Please come.

Five seconds later, another:

I'll pick you up.

And I realize now I have no choice.

I have to go. There's no way to tell him not to come and get me.

But there's something else.

I *want* him to come and get me.

I want to see him again.

And there's another something else.

How does he know where I live?

FIVE.

I ask him when I see him.

I wait by the picture window in the living room and as soon as I see his car pull into my driveway, I'm out the door.

His car is nice. It's a dark blue, shiny, clean.

He gets out to open the door for me, which I don't expect. He's there before I reach the passenger side, and he's wearing a dark blue suit. I'm wearing a dress I've worn to each of my grandparents' funerals. It's black, goes to the knees. I feel weird wearing it. Like maybe it smells. Like somehow it's absorbed the odor of all the funeral parlors it's seen. The formaldehyde. The flowers.

The smell nobody admits is rot.

"You look nice," he says when I reach him.

I shrug and mumble thanks.

I don't like when people give me compliments. It makes me feel like I owe them something in return.

Plus, it's a funeral. Do I really want to look nice for a funeral? People shouldn't look nice for funerals, should they? What does that say about them? Does it say that they don't care about the person that died? That they have enough time to do their hair and their makeup and put appropriate shoes on? Shouldn't we all be too upset to do any of that?

His car smells good. He closes the door for me and I put my seat belt on. He fixes the radio so it's low enough for us to talk and then he pulls out of my driveway and starts off down the road. The funeral is three towns over. I guess it makes sense I didn't know them. Despite what Erie said, it's reasonable I wouldn't know someone who lived three towns over. If they kept to themselves. Didn't go to a lot of parties. I might not know them.

"You're quiet," he says.

It's there again. This pull. This gravity. I realize I'm happy and I don't know why. I feel a degree of happiness I haven't hoped for in years. A calm, a stillness. I'm hoping he gets lost, that we drive around in circles until we both die, stopping only for gas and water when we're thirsty and snacks when we're hungry. I will put my hand on his leg when he drives and he will sing me lullabies when I can't sleep and I realize I've never wanted any of this before. I've never felt a connection to someone like this and I'm wondering if it's real. I don't know why I should feel it now, for Sayer, but it's here and I'm willing it to stay.

"I'm sorry," I reply.

"You don't have to apologize."

"I like being quiet. I guess."

I like being quiet? We both have apples?

"Molly," he says then, and the way he says my name, it stirs something inside me. A memory, maybe, or a suggestion. All I know is that it sounds like he's said my name before. It sounds like he's practiced saying my name in front of a mirror until he got it completely right.

"Yes?"

"I'm really glad you're coming."

"Oh."

"I think my brother would have appreciated it."

"Were you close?"

"We were brothers," he says, and just the way he says it you can tell exactly what he means. We had our disagreements and sometimes we hated each other but he was my brother and someone hit the back tire of his motorcycle and now he is dead. Now we are driving to his funeral and now I have you in my car and now we are making small talk and you shouldn't have worn that dress. The smell of formaldehyde, it is suffocating me.

"Right, of course," I say. I have a brother, too. And Clancy is sad and Clancy is annoying and Clancy murdered all my goldfish when he was seven, picked them out of the bowl by their tails and held them thrashing until their tiny lungs collapsed and I hated him for that. I hated him with the true hatred of a nine-year-old girl, but he is still my brother and my love for him will go beyond death. It will go beyond goldfish and it will go beyond life. And I can't imagine driving to his funeral. In my mind, he will never die. He and Hazel will never die. They will never age and they will remain constant forever.

"I still can't thank you enough," he says. Out of the corner of my eye I see him look out of the corner of his eye at me. I see one finger of his right hand twitch like he would like to take my hand in his hand but he won't. He doesn't.

"I did what anyone would have done," I say. But this is a lie. There were other people there and nobody else did what I did. Nobody let the dying boy cough blood all over them. Nobody held the dying boy's head while he took his last dying breaths. I had to throw my sweater out. My favorite sweater, I pushed it to the bottom of the trash can and then I crumpled up pages of an old newspaper and I threw the pages in the trash until I couldn't see the sweater anymore. Blood doesn't come out. That much blood, it wouldn't have come out and so I didn't even try.

"I don't think there are many people who would have done what you did," Sayer says.

49

And then we're quiet. I look out the window, and everything seems foreign. We might as well be in a different country, a different universe. We might as well be in the future or in the past. Nothing seems familiar to me anymore. The people I used to know are strangers. And the stranger sitting next to me seems like someone I've known my whole life.

I know.

Nothing makes sense to me, either.

And then I ask him. I say, "Sayer, how did you know where I live?"

And he says, "I don't want to lie to you."

And I say, "Why would you lie?"

And he says, "There are reasons."

"What would you lie about?"

"It's a small town," he says. "Anyone could have told me."

"Did someone tell you?"

"At one point," he says, "someone told me."

And I say, "How long have you known me?"

And he says, "It feels like forever."

And I say, "I think it feels like forever, too."

And he says, "No more questions, okay? Not right now."

And I remember his brother has died and so I nod okay and I stare out the window again, and when we get to the funeral parlor I stay in the car while he walks around and opens the door for me. And when he opens the door, he takes my hand and he pulls me out and then he pulls me into a hug and he hugs me like he will die without me. Like I am the only thing keeping him alive. I want to tell him the feeling is mutual but I don't. I don't say anything. Anything I say will come out wrong and so I don't say anything.

The funeral is a blur. I mean, I don't lose time but I force myself to disassociate from my body, to lose concentration, because it's easier to handle. This is something I've gotten very good at doing. I sit in the second row surrounded by strangers. Some of them look at me like they might know me, but that is how they look at everybody and nobody says hi to me. Sayer sits to the side with a man who might be his uncle, a woman who might be his grandmother. The room is small and the casket is closed. But even though it is closed I can see Lyle inside it. I can see Lyle bleeding and I can see Lyle dead. And I can see Lyle reborn and I can see Lyle flying through the air and I can see Lyle on the pavement with blood pouring out of his mouth.

And then I can see something else. And it is like I *am* somewhere else and I am in my car again and I am wearing my favorite gray sweater, the one Lyle bled on. And I am driving too fast and I am looking in my rearview mirror like someone might be following me. I'm trying to lose someone. And I'm crying, but I wipe the tears away from my face and I tell myself I've made the right decision. But what decision have I made?

What decision have I made?

I am in the funeral parlor and when I wake up it's like I'm waking up from something I have lost.

I knew Lyle Avery.

Lyle Avery knew me.

I was with him before he died.

I was with him before he got on the motorcycle.

I knew him.

I was with him and then I left him and I told him not to follow me.

I told him not to follow me, but he did.

And he tried to catch up to me and someone hit the back tire of his motorcycle and he flew over my car but it was not my fault. It was not my fault because I told him not to follow me. It was not my fault because I told him I didn't want him to follow me.

I get up in the middle of a eulogy. Somebody is giving a eulogy for Lyle, but if I do not get out of the room immediately, I will scream.

In the hallway I lean against the wall and I take big giant gulps of air and I force myself to remain present. I can feel myself slipping away, but I press my hands against the wall and I want to stay here. I want to be here. I do not want to miss any more time. This is my time and I do not want to lose it.

And of course I have never met Lyle Avery before. I have never met him before in my life.

"Molly."

I open my eyes and Sayer is right in front of me.

I say, "How did I know your brother?"

And he says, "Let me get through today. Let me just get through today and I will explain everything."

But when he asks me to come inside with him, I say that I can't. I can't go back in there because there are too many people and the walls are moving. They are closing in on me, and he asks if I am okay and suddenly I am not okay. And he looks concerned and he takes my hand in his hand and I think, Please just leave me alone. Please forget that you ever met me. Please just let me be by myself and let me be quiet and let me be still.

"Molly," he says. "Do you want to get some air?"

I nod stiffly. Air, sure. I've left my coat on my chair but suddenly air and cold are all I need. I leave him and walk down the hall as quickly as I can without running, and I burst out of the funeral parlor and it comes back in a rush. It comes back in a rush of color and sound and conversation.

I'm in a building. It is a dirty, abandoned building and I am arguing with someone. I'm arguing with Lyle. Of course, my mind says, I am always arguing with Lyle.

But that doesn't make any sense. I've never met Lyle before.

• • •

This is what happens.

Lyle has a bottle of whiskey in one hand, but it's empty and he throws it against a wall and the bottle breaks into a thousand pieces and I jump backward and I feel scared of him for the first time. And when he sees my face, scared, he stops, and he takes a step away from the wall and he looks at me.

"You're scared of me," he says.

"I'm not scared of you, Lyle. Right now you're scaring me a little, yes, but I'm not scared of you."

"I'm not going to hurt you. I just . . . Jesus, you can be such a . . ."

He paces a tight circle. I'm angry. I'm angry with him.

"Such a *what*, Lyle?" He doesn't answer. I can tell he's not going to answer.

I'm so angry now that I can't stay still. I turn and walk away from him and then I come back and then I walk away and then I come back, and then he grabs my arm to get me to stay in one place.

"You know," he says.

"Know what?"

"How much you mean to me."

"Sure," I say. "Yeah, I know how much I mean to you."

"But that doesn't change anything?"

"It changes everything," I say. "You know that it changes everything."

"It doesn't change everything," he says. "It doesn't change your mind."

"I can't help it," I say. It's more like I beg. Like I plead.

"You can try. Maybe you're just not trying hard enough."

"You'd like me to try? You'd like me to *try* to be in love with you? Do you hear how that sounds?"

"That's not what I meant."

"It sounded like that's what you meant."

"I'm not asking you to . . . Fuck, how can you possibly . . . You don't even know him!"

"I know him. Of course I know him."

"But you forget him. All the time. You're constantly forgetting him. How can you love someone you can't even remember?"

It's a low blow and I answer with an equally low blow.

"I forget you, too. As soon as you're out of my sight, Lyle, I forget you."

He looks like he wants to hit me. All this anger he has crawling underneath his skin, how have I never seen it before?

"Look, I can't do this anymore. I can't stay here any longer. I'm missing school for this, Lyle. You said this was important."

He yells, "THIS IS IMPORTANT!"

"You said it couldn't wait. It could have waited. I can't afford to miss any more school."

His face softens a little. He looks around at the pieces of the whiskey bottle. Like he wishes they could gather themselves up and mold themselves together and fill themselves up again. I imagine him offering a toast to me. I don't know what else he would toast to.

"You don't even know him," he says. His voice is quiet. His eyes will not meet mine.

"I know him," I say. "You know I know him."

"And there's nothing I can say?"

There's no emotion anymore. His voice, it's flat.

"You've said everything."

"So there's nothing I can say?"

"I have to go."

"You're going?"

"Yeah."

"You're just going to go?"

"That's what people do. They go."

"Or they stay."

"Yes. They stay in abandoned buildings forever. Grow up. Have kids. Paint murals."

"We wouldn't have to stay here."

He's so sincere and his sincerity makes me uncomfortable. I don't know what to do with it. I don't know where to put it.

"Don't you want him to be happy?" I say. I don't know where these words come from; they jump to my throat and escape before I can stop them.

He looks like he's thinking about it. He actually looks like he's considering it. The happiness of another human being. Does it matter to him? Does it mean anything?

"No," he says. "Not about this. This is mine."

"Jesus, I'm not a conquest."

"But I—"

"It doesn't matter. It's over. It doesn't matter."

"It should," he says and you can see him regret it immediately.

He should regret it immediately.

He's a child and he's an asshole and there are a million things I could say to him, but I don't say anything.

I turn and walk away.

He says my name once, choking, pleading, and I don't turn around. I say, "Don't follow me, Lyle," and I leave the warehouse. I walk past his motorcycle and I get in my car and I drop my phone underneath the seat, but I don't bend down to pick it up because it's better if I can't answer him. If he calls me, I don't want to answer him.

I look up at the warehouse and for a second I can see him in one of the windows, but then he's gone, he's backed away, and in some corner of my mind I realize he's going to follow me. He loves me and I don't love him and he thinks he can change my mind. He thinks you can convince someone to love you.

I drive too fast. I want to get away from here; I need to get back to school. I don't know why I came at all. I shouldn't have come. I should have learned by now that Lyle isn't Lyle anymore. He's not my friend. He's something else. When someone falls in love with you like that, he stops being your friend. He stops caring about your friendship and he only cares about wanting you to love him back.

I'm on Water Street when I feel myself slipping. Receding, fading.

I look in the rearview mirror. There I am. I look just like Molly. I am Molly. My name is Molly. Molly's family is my family. Molly's life is my life. Molly's mistakes are my mistakes.

Only she doesn't have to live with them.

I do.

SIX.

Sayer finds me on a bench outside the funeral parlor. It's cold. I'm cold. My teeth are chattering and he has to pull me up. My legs are stiff. He promises coffee inside. It's not the best coffee, he says, but it's hot. Just come inside. We're almost done. We don't have to go to the burial. I will take you home. You can go to sleep early. Are you tired? You look tired. Just come and have some coffee and then I will bring you home.

He leads me into a little sitting room that is empty of any dead people, any closed coffins. He gets me a cup of coffee and then he disappears somewhere.

The coffee's effect is almost instantaneous. I feel life

returning to my veins, blood speeding up, my heart pumping gratefully. My fingers are slowly thawing out. It's been a warm October so far. When did it get so cold?

I drink the whole thing and then I get up and stretch and find a garbage can. It's filled halfway with identical paper cups. The last dregs of greasy, bitter coffee. I drop mine in with the others and watch it settle. What I saw outside, what I remembered or what I dreamed up or what I fabricated, it's begging to be considered. It's right there inside my veins and it's crawling under my skin and it's looking for a way to come up to the surface. But I don't want it to. I mean, I don't want to think about it. Not right now. Because I don't know what it means and I don't know if it's the truth and I don't know anything. I feel like I don't know anything anymore. I feel like I'm going crazy.

When Sayer comes back into the room, he puts his hand on my hip but then he pulls his hand away and I think how every time he pulls his hand away from me I want to grab it back. He's ready to drive me home now, but I don't want to go home. I don't want Lyle put into the ground without me there because he was my friend. I knew him. Somehow, I knew him. I loved him. I loved him like he was my best friend and that wasn't enough for him but that's not my fault. You can't decide how much you love people. It just happens. If you have to think about it, then it's not really real.

"I want to go to the cemetery."

"You don't have to," he says.

"Was he my friend, Sayer? Can you tell me if he was my friend?"

There's a long sort of quiet that stretches out over us, and as much as I am confused—as much as I am scared and as much as my body is humming with a careful, waiting energy—I feel okay as long as Sayer looks at me. As long as his breathing wraps around my body, as long as I am held in his sway, cloaked in his quiet: I am okay. I don't know why I am okay but I am okay.

"He was your friend," he says finally.

"But why don't I remember?"

"Maybe you're starting to."

"And you?"

"Me?"

"Do I know you, too?"

He smiles. I don't know what kind of smile it is. It's not a smile of happiness or a smile of understanding. Maybe it's more like a grimace.

"No. We've never met," he says.

And I don't know if I believe him, but what can I say? I can't say anything. I don't remember.

At the cemetery it is only me and Sayer and the pallbearers who've come from the funeral parlor to lower Lyle's body into the ground. Sayer parks his car and we walk behind their truck as they drive slowly through the graves. The day has turned even colder and my breath comes out in puffs of gray. Sayer walks one or two paces to my left. For whatever reason, I feel like this is some sort of decision. A decision to keep his distance from me, maybe, or a decision to at least be aware of every inch between us.

This is my fifth funeral, my fifth burial. When my grandparents died, I was sad but it was an inevitable sadness, an obligatory grief. I walked through graves like these graves; all cemeteries look the same. I clung to my mother's dress as they lowered her mother into the ground but that was only because she was crying, my mother, and I felt her sadness like an extension of my own sadness. I felt her loss more palpably than my own loss. When her father died, it was the same, but when my paternal grandparents were put into the ground, a week apart, I stood back from my parents and was terrified by the grief of my father. I had never seen him cry. And when his father died, I thought he might never stop. I thought once those gates were open, they would never close again. They could never be closed again. How could they, when he was so sad? When his eyes were so red? When his throat was so choked?

With Lyle it is different. But it is confusing. It doesn't make sense; it's cloudy and incomplete. I still have no idea what I saw, what those memories mean and whether they are real or completely made up or some mixture of truth and lies, but at least one thing is clear to me now. I knew Lyle. In some way, I knew him. I know that I loved him, but I know also that at least some part of me resented him. Where that resentment comes from, I don't know, but I can't deny that I feel it now. I can't deny that it's bubbled to the surface, that it's clawing around for an explanation.

But I feel like I should be devastated. Or that I am devastated, and I just can't work out the reason why. But it's there, at least, and when we reach his grave and there is the big empty hole they will put his casket into, I am crying. I am sobbing. I am fading.

I only lose a little while. Fifteen minutes, twenty. The hole is half filled up with dirt and I can't see anything left of Lyle's casket. Sayer is looking at me worriedly. Or expectantly. Or with concern. I don't know. I hope I haven't done anything to give myself away, said anything strange, or just stared unseeing into the sky while maybe Sayer tried to talk to me but got no answer. But if I can fool my whole family, my best friends, then I can fool a stranger.

"Headache," I mumble, pressing my fingers against my temples. This might explain any outward weirdness, at least, and it has the distinct advantage of being the truth. I can feel the dull throb starting low in the back of my throat, working its way steadily upward. There is a metallic taste in my mouth and my tongue is slippery and I realize I must have bitten it at some point. I'm still crying and the tears are thick on my cheeks.

But this isn't fair. Lyle wasn't my brother, he was Sayer's, and I am hogging all of his sadness. I take a step back, a physical step, and after a few more minutes the pallbearers have finished covering the hole and they leave without saying anything. I don't know what they would have said, anyway, but they're gone and it's just Sayer and me and Sayer has dropped to his knees in front of the grave.

I let him stay there, shoulders heaving, and I study the backs of my hands to keep myself from fading out again. My fingernail polish is chipping and I focus on the color, focus on the broken nail on my left index finger. Sometimes it works like this. If I feel it threatening, pulling the edges of my consciousness, I can repress it. Keep my mind busy, keep myself occupied. Stay here.

Even as I am quiet, even as I watch Sayer grieve, I am remembering.

The drive to the warehouse. The text message from Lyle asking me to meet him. My response, *I'm at school*. His answer, *It's important*.

But isn't everything with Lyle important? Or—wasn't it?

That was part of his charm, and part of the reason I was almost constantly annoyed with him. Everything was always so important. Any thought that occurred to him, any emotion he felt took precedence over whatever somebody else might be feeling. He had room for compassion, for understanding, of course, but at his most basic level he would always think of himself first. He would always have trouble understanding how to relate to people because it was in his nature to keep them at arm's length. To dismiss them.

That's the reason he couldn't understand why I didn't love him.

He was so used to it.

So attractive and so dark and so interesting, I really think I was the first girl who wanted to keep him as a friend. He was a brother to me, my adopted family. But I never wanted more. Never even considered it. That would be too easy, too expected. He meant more to me than that.

I remember this now.

I step forward and put my hand on Sayer's shoulder. He's stopped crying, and a few times he shakes his head like he has no idea what he is supposed to do now. I wonder what happened to his parents, why none of his family came to the burial. I wonder why Lyle's pallbearers were strangers. I wonder why Sayer didn't help lower his brother into the ground. And I wonder how close they really were. I can sense a tension between them, but surely that has dissipated in death. Sibling rivalry can only go so far.

Sayer's shoulder is warm. I spread my fingers and he lifts his arm and puts his hand on top of mine.

"Now everyone's dead," he says.

There's nothing I can say to this, and so I squeeze his shoulder and he squeezes my hand in return and I wonder how true that is. Does he have no one left now? No cousins? No grandparents? What about those people sitting next to him in the funeral parlor? How close is he to them? Will he live with them now? I don't even know how old Sayer is. He might have graduated high school; he looks like he could be old enough. Maybe he already lives on his own. Maybe he lived with Lyle. Could he have been Lyle's guardian? Was he old enough? Would Lyle's death have implications reaching far beyond the usual mourning? Was Sayer free now? Had Lyle always held him back from a normal life?

I'm reaching, maybe.

When I don't know what to do, I reach.

Sayer stands up. He looks so similar to Lyle, but he's different. They're different in every way. Sayer said we never met before but even in the short time I've known him, I know he's different from the only memory I have of Lyle. His eyes are kinder. They are less sharp and accusing, a darker green. His skin less pale. His hair cut shorter. He is taller. Less gangly. Warmer.

Where with Lyle you are always kept on the outside, worming your way closer through dirt and mud and sticks and rocks, with Sayer you are as close as you can stand. You are on top of him; you are within him. He wraps himself around your body; he uses you as a core. You become his center. You are a part of him, and he makes you feel like the better part. I feel like the better part of him and I don't think I've ever felt like the better part of anything.

That's just how he is. He puts people before him. Pushes you forward, if he has to, but he never lets you sink into the shadows.

"I'll drive you home," he says.

He drives me home.

I spend the car ride looking out the window, trying not to furrow my brow so much, trying to convince myself that this is okay, that I am okay, that it is time for me to go home now. Sayer seems equally intent on not saying anything; we could be in two separate cars for all the silence. Once or twice he sniffs or clears his throat, and I look over at him quickly and there are tears that never really stop. I wonder how long he'll be sad. I wonder if his sadness will last forever, stretching on like an ocean. Drowning everyone he cares about. Drowning people he doesn't even know. He won't be able to control it. Oceans ebb and flow as they wish. They cover everything. They make everything blue.

At my house he parks on the street and he gets out of the car and I know I'm supposed to wait for him to come around and open my door for me. And when he does, I take his hand and I practically throw myself into his arms and then I remember he was supposed to explain everything to me. He was supposed to tell me how I knew his brother, why I don't remember anything, why Lyle died trying to catch up to me.

It's like he can hear my thoughts. He pulls away from

me and says, "I'd like to see you again."

"Tuesday?" I say. "Wednesday?"

Every day. All of the days. Today, tomorrow.

"Tuesday, sure," he says. "I'll call you."

"Are you okay? I mean, are you going to be okay?"

"I'll be okay," he says. "My brother and I weren't close."

"But he was your brother."

"He was my brother, yes. But he was not the easiest person to know."

"Did I know that?" I say. I wish I hadn't said it but sometimes I can't stop myself.

"You knew that," he says.

He puts a hand on the side of my face and he leans in and kisses my forehead. I think, why am I still standing? My legs have surely given out; my muscles have withered and dried up and disappeared. And people without muscles can't stand. They can only sink into the pavement. They can only collapse and lie helpless on the grass.

"I'll call you."

He walks around the car again and gets in the driver's side and I watch him pull away from the curb. I feel sick to my stomach. Like I might throw up. When I turn toward the house, there's movement in the living room window. A curtain falling back into place. And I think, oh great, they'll ask me about it now. Was that the brother? How was the funeral? Why did he kiss you on the forehead and why do you look like you're about to throw up?

But inside, nobody says anything. I go up to my room and I lie down on the bed and all I see is Lyle's face on the ceiling of my room. Lyle's face on the inside of my eyelids.

Lyle, dead.

Lyle throwing a whiskey bottle against a wall.

Sayer driving me home.

Sayer kissing my forehead.

And I don't know where to put any of it, so I let it swirl around until I fall asleep. I fall asleep and I dream of green eyes. Gravestones. A hand on someone's shoulder and my forehead, burning and hot.

SEVEN.

I can't put off seeing my friends any longer and so I agree
to meet Luka and Erie for lunch the next day.

I don't want to go. I have to pull myself out of bed in
the morning, and while I'm in the shower Hazel lays out
clothes for me on my bed. She does this sometimes; she
wants to be a clothing designer when she's older. She thinks
I'm mostly a lost cause, but she always manages to make me
look presentable. I get dressed quickly and blow-dry my
hair for as long as I can stand it (it's too hot, I'm too bored,
my hair is too long), then I brush on some mascara and I'm
out the door before anyone can ask me where I'm going.
But there's Hazel perched on the hood of my car, wearing

an enormous oversized sweater and reading a book.

"Need a ride somewhere?" I say, standing in front of her. She looks adorable, my sister, with her pixie haircut and her black velvet leggings and clunky lace-up boots. She could wear a carpet wrapped around her body and still manage to make it look put together. She's even wearing lipstick—her favorite pale pink. She had me try it on once and I looked like a clown. Even she admitted that.

"Homeward bound," she answers. She taps the hood next to her, but I'm not sure it will hold both of us so I just take a step closer. She lowers her book, saves the place with a finger. Pushes her sunglasses onto the top of her head. "You look nice."

"Thanks to you," I say.

She shrugs. There's something there, behind that shrug. I don't know what it is.

"Where are you headed?" she asks.

"Lunch with Luka and Erie."

"Oh, that's nice."

"Sure. You?"

"Reading," she says, and lifts the book. "For school. Bookstore, later."

"Yeah, I'll be there, too. Register duty."

"Restocking."

"And Clancy?" I say. I haven't seen him this morning.

"Sleeping," she says.

The only person who can sleep longer than I can.

"Sure you don't need a ride somewhere?" I ask. I'm getting this feeling like she wants to tell me something but she's certainly taking her time, whatever it is.

"I saw you with that boy yesterday," she says, sliding off the car, stretching her legs, one after the other.

The mystery curtain mover.

"The brother," I say. "Of the boy who died."

"I figured," she says. "How was the funeral?"

"Fine," I say. "Sad."

I don't know, how are funerals? What are you supposed to say about them? The flowers were nice? The casket was closed? Everyone cried and I remembered that I knew him somehow? That we were friends and that I was with him at a warehouse before he died?

"Are you going to see him again?" she asks.

"Am I going to . . ."

"I was just wondering."

"Oh, yeah. Maybe, I think so."

"Do you think that's a good idea?"

I guess I haven't thought about it.

Is it a bad idea?

I want answers. And he said he had them.

"It's an okay idea."

I settle for this.

"Sure," she says.

The way she says *sure*. It's like she wants to say more, but this time I know she's not going to. She's too thoughtful;

her face is too set. She's made up her mind.

"What does that mean?" I ask.

"It means sure," she says, smiling, ducking out of my way before I can say anything else or reach out and stop her. "Okay. All right. Sounds good."

"Hazel," I say. She pauses on the steps that lead around the side of the house and up to the front door.

"Yeah, Molly," she responds. She turns around, taps her glasses down over her eyes.

"Do you know something I don't know?"

She falters briefly, opens her mouth to respond, cocks her head like she's forgotten her words halfway through saying them. She finally smiles.

"What about you, Molly? Do you know something I don't know?"

A standstill. An impasse.

She smiles wider.

She turns and skips up the steps. Like a fairy. Like a sprite.

I meet Luka and Erie in the parking lot of a local diner called Sal's. It's basically the only place in town not overrun by tourists. It's out of the way. You have to come here on purpose.

As soon as I'm out of the car, Erie grabs my hand and pulls me into the diner like she'll die if she goes another moment without food. Like I said: metabolism of a hummingbird.

Something equally small and blurry.

Luka brings up the rear, shuffling his feet. I swing my arm behind me to hit him but come up with only air.

"She told me everything," he says when we sit down. We're at a table in the back.

"Didn't think you'd mind," Erie explains, largely unapologetic. "How was the funeral?"

I'm still not sure how to answer that question. I sort of shrug. Why do people ask about funerals? And what are you supposed to say about them?

I settle for "Fine. It was fine."

"How's the brother?" Erie asks.

"Sort of good, I guess." And then, because I can tell they aren't at all satisfied with my lackluster recounting of events, I add, "He's sad. I mean—obviously. He was just really sad. And it was . . . I mean, hardly anyone showed up. Or, people showed up but it just didn't really seem . . . it doesn't really seem like they have much family."

Erie makes a sympathetic noise in the back of her throat and Luka looks uncomfortable, and then the waitress comes over and we all order our food and gradually Erie fills up all the empty air with conversation about her weekend, about her poet boyfriend, about her unwillingness to finish Mr. Stone's English essay. Luka systematically ignores my repeated attempts at making eye contact while attacking his grilled cheese and tomato sandwich. Luka isn't good with stuff like this. When my last grandparent died, he avoided me for two weeks. Finally I followed him into the boys' bathroom and refused to let him out of the stall until he acknowledged me.

I move my salad around on my plate until I realize it's quiet and Erie is looking at me like I'm supposed to say something now. I try and respond but inhale awkwardly and choke on a cherry tomato, cutting off my oxygen for the next twenty seconds while I cough like a fool. Blinking back tears, I wipe my face with a napkin and take a careful sip of water.

"Really, Molly," Erie says, rolling her eyes.

"I didn't hear what you said," I tell her.

"I asked if you're going to see him again."

"See him? See who?" I say too quickly. It comes out awkward and I feel my face grow hot. Erie rolls her eyes again. She's pretty good at rolling her eyes. Lots of practice.

"What's his name again?" Luka asks.

"Sayer," Erie says.

"Oh, him," I say. This comes out wrong, too. It was supposed to be more offhanded.

"Weird name," Luka says.

"You have a weird name," Erie says.

"You have a weird name," Luka says. Under his breath, he says something that sounds like *moon*. Erie pushes her shoulder into his shoulder.

"Well, are you?" she says, turning her attention back to me.

"Maybe. I mean, I don't know. I mean, maybe."

"Well, that clears it up," Luka says.

"I guess maybe, yes," I say. "I mean, probably. He said we should see each other again."

A tiny thrill. Saying the words out loud. Sayer wants to see me again.

Erie takes a sip of water and they both wait for me to continue.

"I said yes."

Erie smiles, letting her shoulders fall as she leans across the table, closer to me. "Finally," she says.

"What do you mean finally?" I say.

"I mean like, I thought we were going to have to sit here forever before you admitted that you're going to see this guy again."

"Your support is endearing," I say.

"I don't think she meant that," Luka says to Erie.

"No, really, I'm happy you and Sayer hit it off," Erie continues. "This has to be a difficult time for him and he's lucky to have you."

"Yeah, sure," I say. "He seems nice."

"Of course he's nice," Erie responds. "Why wouldn't he be nice?"

"When are you seeing him?" Luka asks.

"Tuesday."

"What are you going to do?" Erie asks.

"I don't know. He's going to call me."

"Great," Luka says. "Super."

"What does that mean?" I ask him.

"It's just like. Great. You're both going to have boy-friends now."

"Oh god, no, it's not like that," I say quickly. Erie is beaming and staring off into space, probably planning our eventual double wedding. "Erie," I say. She looks at me, surprised. "No. Stop. No."

She shrugs. "It's a possibility."

Luka exhales loudly and pushes his plate away from him. "I have to get a girlfriend now. I have to call some people. Molly, you never date anyone. You're putting a lot of pressure on me."

"I don't *never* date," I say.

"Last boyfriend: Will Bonnet. Sixth grade," Erie recites.

"That was not my last—"

"Nope, Alan doesn't count."

"His last name was Bonnet? Like, a bonnet?" Luka asks, putting his hands on his head like a cap.

"Alan counts," I say weakly.

"Like a hat?" Luka persists.

"It was a week; Alan doesn't count."

"It's French, Luka. Like—*bonn-ay.*"

"Is that—really?" Erie asks.

"That's what he said," I say, shrugging.

"Whatever. He counts. Alan doesn't count. Luka, we'll still sit you with at lunch," Erie says. She puts a hand on

Luka's arm. He shrugs.

"Everyone is getting vastly ahead of themselves," I say.

"You think he's cute," Erie says. "He wants to see you again."

"Don't you think it's a little weird, though?" Luka says. "I mean, you were the last person to see his brother, right?"

Lyle Avery's face flashes in front of my eyes. But it's not his face in the warehouse. This is something else.

"He seems nice," Erie says. "It's not weird."

"I mean, I'm not saying she shouldn't go. I'm just saying it's a little weird."

"It's not weird. It's sweet. I think it's sweet."

I blink my eyes and Lyle's face is gone. Erie and Luka are totally absorbed in the back-and-forth of whether or not seeing Sayer again is a creepy thing or a good thing and I feel suddenly nauseous, suddenly sick.

"Hey," I say, but it doesn't come out loud enough and neither of them hears me. Erie has her hand on Luka's arm again and she's trying to convince him about something I don't understand because my ears are ringing and I taste something bitter in the back of my throat. I wait until they're done talking and then I say it again, louder, "Hey," and this time Luka hears me and he puts a hand over Erie's mouth to shut her up and she pushes it away, laughing.

"What?" she says. "What's wrong?"

"I have to go," I say. I dig around my purse and find a ten-dollar bill. I hold it out to them and wave it around until Luka takes it.

"What's wrong?"

"Nothing. Nothing, it's just—I forgot about the bookstore. I told my dad I'd stop by. Big shipment. Things to, you know, put away. Catalog."

"You usually go in later than this," Luka says.

"Sorry. I just told him I would. I forgot."

"Are you sure? You just got here," Erie says.

"I'm sure. I'm sorry. I'll call you."

I jump out of my seat and grab my purse and try to keep myself from running toward the door.

I barely make it into my car before my vision turns to fiery white and my ears rush with blood and I'm not in my car anymore.

I'm leaning against an enormous oak tree on the edge of the graveyard in town. It's a seaside graveyard; I taste salt on my tongue. You get so used to it living in Manchester that sometimes you don't even notice it. After a storm it is particularly strong.

So it's stormed recently.

The skies are still gray.

I'm reading a book and I have a coat on. Jeans and sneakers.

I'm waiting for someone, and when he gets there I smile. It's a real smile. He sits down next to me and puts his arm around my shoulders and I lean my head against his arm.

"Took you long enough," I say.

I said.

This is before, of course.

Before the accident and before the argument in the warehouse.

Before the whiskey bottle and the shattered glass.

This is the last thing I can't remember.

I am here, leaning against this oak tree, leaning my head on Lyle's arm.

I am always leaning on something.

EIGHT.

The next day at school I move through the hallways like they're flooded. Like I'm swimming through them, coming up every so often for air and clawing my way through seaweed that would hold me down, choke me, suffocate me. My lungs burn with the effort of breathing. What I wouldn't do for gills. At my locker I press my forehead into the door and let the metal cool me down. Erie and Luka keep their distance, treading just close enough so it can't be said they're avoiding me. I appreciate the tact. I also appreciate the distance.

After lunch my headache's gotten so bad I skip class and visit the nurse. She's notoriously stingy with the pain pills and I have to beg her for two ibuprofens. She gives them to me with a look of obvious distaste, but let her distaste me all she wants. I have the pills.

Then she does something I'm not expecting. She watches me take the pills, gets me the glass of water and everything, and when I'm done she puts a hand on the side of my face. Not checking for a temperature, exactly, maybe just checking for a pulse. For warmth. The giveaway signs of life.

"Are you all right, Molly?" she asks.

"Fine," I say. I'm fine. I'm fine. I'm fine.

"Would you like to call someone?"

She lets me use the phone in her office and Alex answers with a mouth full of food. Lunchtime. I find myself unable to properly articulate my words and after a few seconds of grunts and heavy sighs, I manage a strained hello.

"Molly? Is that you?"

I hear him swallow and wait for me to answer him.

"Yeah, it's me."

"Is everything okay?"

In one year of steady meetings—three times a week for the first four months and now just on Wednesdays—I have never, ever called Alex. I've had his number memorized since that first week and I have dialed it on two separate occasions but I hung up before it was able to connect.

No.

Not everything is okay.

In fact, I can think of absolutely nothing that is deserving of the label "okay."

I can't answer him. I turn my back to the windows that line one wall of the nurse's office and I stare blindly, seeing nothing.

Lyle and me sitting underneath an oak tree.

But I've never met Lyle before, my mind screams.

"Molly?"

"Alex," I say, and his name catches in my throat.

"When can you get here?" he says.

I mumble something into the phone. I can't remember what I mumble. I'm forgetting everything as soon as it happens. I say something to the nurse and she lets me leave, but I can't remember what I say to her. I go to my locker and I get my coat and my keys and I have the vague idea that I shouldn't be driving. I shouldn't be driving, but Clancy won't be sixteen for another few months and I can't call my parents. What would I tell them?

I can't ask Erie or Luka to skip classes.

Pull yourself together, Molly. You can drive to the doctor.

It's sunny but cold outside. I make my way to the car and the air outside helps clear my head a little, lifts me up from the constant dreams of drowning. For a minute I entertain the idea of finding Sayer leaning against my car again, without the umbrella this time, a slow smile spreading across his face when he sees me.

But of course nobody's there.

I drive slower than usual and I keep the windows rolled down, and the breeze hitting my face leaves me red cheeked and puffing, but I'm glad for it. It keeps me here. It keeps me present.

It's a short drive to Alex's office and he's waiting outside for me. I didn't expect that. I think back to how I must have sounded on the phone and I'm sure I scared him. I haven't talked about suicide in a while, but it was there once. That was the entire reason I started going to him, wasn't it? An offhand comment made to Clancy, overheard by Hazel, related quickly to my parents. And there I was. Dumped unceremoniously in Alex's office. He wasn't like any therapist I'd seen on TV or imagined for myself. He listened when I talked and it seemed like he actually cared about what happened to me. He became a sort of friend, didn't he? He had become a presence in my life. Someone to talk to when there was no one else. If I had asked him to come pick me up at school, he would have, wouldn't he? It hadn't occurred to me but he would have. Of course he would have.

I haven't gotten out of my car and after a few minutes he comes over and opens the door for me. I realize I'm crying. I'm losing tiny bits of my memory at a time. I don't remember turning my car off. I don't remember covering my face with my hands. I'm living disjointed. I'm living in bits.

I have to tell him or it will never stop.

Maybe I've finally realized that.

I get out of the car, declining his help, and I trip and almost fall into him but I still won't let him hold my arm. I sniff until I stop crying and I walk ahead of him, leaving him to lock up my car, make sure I've taken my keys, my purse. He shuts the door. Follows me.

In his office I fall down into the armchair and he sits on the desk.

The rest of the memory wasn't anything special. Lyle and I stayed underneath the oak tree for a while and we were friends. We talked. And a few times there was almost an air of forced calm, of purposeful peace between us. A tension we were trying hard to move past.

But then he said something and I said something and he didn't like what I said. He got up and left. Maybe he asked me something, but I can't hear what he asked me and I can't hear what I answered. But he didn't like it. Whatever it was, he didn't like my answer and he looked at me for a couple of seconds and I looked down at my hands and then he got up and left.

Well, that would make sense.

The next time we saw each other we fought, didn't we? He told me he loved me at some point. I told him I couldn't think about him that way. Those things, at least, had fallen into place.

Alex is waiting for me to say something. I look up at him and there's that look again. That look I've been seeing on everyone's faces lately.

It's like they're waiting for something.

It's like they're waiting for me to do something.

"I haven't told you everything," I say. I don't know where it comes from, this sudden desire to tell Alex the truth, but it's like I've reached the genius conclusion that he can't help me if I'm not honest with him. I've pretended I was okay. I've been an idiot.

"What haven't you told me?"

"Last year. When I told my brother I was thinking it would be easier. On everybody. To, you know."

I can't bring myself to say it.

To kill myself.

To end my life.

To walk out into the ocean or slit my wrists in the bathtub.

"When your troubles started," Alex supplies.

"My troubles, yeah. Something else started back then, too."

He raises one eyebrow and then lowers it. His face is covered with that look. I don't know what that look means, but to be fair, he's marginally better at hiding it than everyone else.

Marginally.

He moves a hand. Continue.

"Sometimes I can't remember things," I say. My voice is all wrong. Too quiet. Too angular. The words are hard and the edges are sharp. They hit my teeth and my head aches with the resounding click of them.

"What kind of things can't you remember?"

It seems stupid, right, asking me about what I can't remember. But it's like maybe he knows. It's like maybe he knows that all these things I've lost, they've started to come back to me.

"Blocks of time," I begin. "I'll be doing something and then a couple hours have passed. Or a couple minutes, even. Or half a day. I'll sort of . . . wake up, somewhere. With no idea of what I've been doing. Where I've been."

I'm struggling to keep my breathing even. I've never spoken this aloud before and it feels like I'm divulging some dirty, awful secret.

Alex lowers his eyes.

I'm expecting him to say something, but he doesn't say anything. He doesn't even look at me.

"Alex?" I say.

He raises his eyes slightly, not his head. "Yes, Molly?"

"Did you hear me?"

"Yes, I did."

"And you're not saying anything. You don't even look . . . surprised, really. And that boy who got killed, the one who knew my name. I'm remembering things about him. I think I knew him. I think all this time I'm missing has something to do with him."

Silence again. Alex gets up. Goes over to the window.

Moves the blinds aside and looks out over the parking lot.

What the fuck is his problem?

"Alex!" I say, sharply this time. He turns around. Looks at me. "Can you say something? I just told you something sort of . . . I mean, I'm missing time, Alex. For a year. Blackouts. Minutes, hours . . . just gone."

I've prepared myself for a lot. For disbelief. For doubt. For questions. For hesitations.

I have not prepared myself for what comes out of Alex's mouth next.

"Molly," he says. "I know."

NINE.

I squeak.

I mean I actually squeak. I open my mouth to say something and nothing comes out except a pathetic, mouse-like exhalation. I'm looking at Alex like he has two heads, like he just breathed fire, like he sprouted fangs and proclaimed the existence of vampires and then sprinted across the room and tore my jugular out. Like he's literally dangling my jugular in front of my face. The pendulum on a clock. Swinging it back and forth. My jugular dripping blood onto the carpet, onto my shoes.

I'm stuck now because I realize I don't know what a jugular looks like. I've always imagined it as a sort of spring, but I doubt that's right. It's a vein, isn't it? Just a normal vein.

He moves away from the window.

"Molly, listen," he begins, wringing his hands in front of him. Is he nervous? He looks nervous. I'm confused. I can't seem to shut my mouth. "Listen, Molly, there's a lot we should talk about."

"We should talk about . . . a lot. There is a lot we should talk about." I repeat this sort of like a robot, which to me seems a fair step above rodent.

"You've been missing chunks of time. Ending up in places and not knowing how you got there."

"That's what I just said. I just said that." Now my voice is hollow. My voice is like a tipped-over tree that's hollowed out. A family of raccoons lives in my voice.

"You've told me before," he says gently. He sits down on the desk again. He looks at me.

"I've never told you that before." The family of raccoons eats garbage for dinner. Garbage for lunch.

"You have. You just don't remember," he clarifies.

Oh.

I guess that makes sense.

I've missed our appointments before, haven't I? Or I've blacked out in the middle of them and woken up hours later, doing my homework or brushing my teeth.

But if I've told him before, why hasn't he ever brought it up again? Ever reminded me?

I'm about to ask him this when he says, "I've tried to tell you. When you're yourself. But you never remember. I've tried to remind you what you've told me, Molly, but you block it all out."

Oh.

That makes sense.

Does it make sense?

I've been having a hard time lately, figuring out what makes sense and what doesn't make sense. What I should question and what I should accept.

"Tell me now," I demand. "Tell me what I've told you."

"I don't think it works like that," he says. "I think I understand it now a bit better. I think you have to work it out yourself."

Oh my god.

I'm crazy.

"I'm crazy."

"You are *not* crazy, Molly. Okay? Molly? You're not crazy."

"I'm not crazy."

I'm not?

I feel crazy.

I feel like I'm losing it.

My handle on reality.

I never thought I had a particularly strong handle on reality, but I guess you can only evaluate something like that once it's threatened.

"Why is this happening to me?" I whisper.

"I don't think I can tell you," he says. "I don't think you'll remember."

"But you know."

"I know, yes."

"What if you write it down?"

"You'll lose the paper."

"What if you sneak up on me and yell it in my ear?"

"I've tried telling you. Molly. I think you have to work it out on your own. You said you remembered something? Something to do with Lyle?"

"Do you know Lyle?"

"I've heard about Lyle."

"He's dead. I saw him die."

"I know."

"I knew him. We were friends."

"I know."

"You know?"

"Yes, I know you were friends."

"How do you know that?"

"You told me, Molly. Tell me what you remembered."

So I tell him. I tell him about the warehouse and the whiskey bottle and I tell him about the oak tree. About sitting underneath the oak tree by the graveyard by the ocean. After a storm. The smell of salt. How I told Lyle something that made him angry—that made him leave. How I can't remember exactly what I told him, but I think it has to do with not being in love with him. That's a guess, but that's what it feels like.

"Now tell me," I say. "Tell me why this is happening."

"It won't work," he says.

"I can stop it. I can stay here."

He sighs; he doesn't want to tell me. But he has to. I can stay here now. I can listen. I can remember.

"Call me later," he says. "Anytime. Let me know you're okay."

"Fine, fine," I say, anxious. "Tell me."

Watching TV. That is what I'm doing when I wake up. Hazel is on the couch next to me and she looks at me with mild interest when I pull myself, irritated, to my feet.

"The phone is there," she says, pointing to the coffee table.

"How did you know—"

"You're supposed to call Alex. It's late."

"He said I could call him whenever," I snap.

"So here," she says, picking up the phone and handing it to me, "call him."

"Are Mom and Dad home?"

"Nope."

"Clancy?"

"Upstairs," she says.

There are tricks to keeping it a secret.

You wake up hours later sitting in front of a TV and you

gather whatever facts you can about whatever it is you've been doing.

"And, um, what are we watching?" I ask.

Hazel smiles. It's a sad smile. She looks at me like she wants to hug me, but she doesn't move.

"*Criminal Minds*," she says. "You like this show."

"I know," I mumble. "I know I like this show."

I take the phone to the backyard and dial Alex's number. It's his office number, the only one I know, but after so many rings it connects directly to his cell phone. He'll be able to see it's me calling. My family's name on the caller ID.

"Molly," he says. He sounds relieved. "It is you, isn't it?"

"Who else would it be?" I ask.

"Right, of course."

A silence. I'm supposed to say something. With Alex, you always have to talk first.

"Guess you were right."

"It's not about being right."

"Maybe, sure. But you were."

"I suppose I was."

"I guess we'll try again sometime."

"Of course."

"You think I have to, what? Figure it out by myself?"

"If you're starting to remember, it might not be so far off."

"Sure, right."

Another silence.

I have a headache. It's turning into a migraine. I can feel it pulling at the edges of my eyes. Pulling at the surface of my skin. Sucking everything inward.

"Well," I say. "See you Wednesday."

"You're okay?"

Are you suicidal, Molly?

Are you thinking of hurting yourself, Molly?

Should we put you back on medication, Molly?

"I'm fine, Alex. Thanks."

"Night or day," he says.

Night or day.

That's what he said the first time he gave me his phone number.

"Anytime," he said. "You can call me anytime, night or day."

"I remember."

I hang up the phone.

My head hurts.

In the kitchen, Hazel waits with a small pill and a glass of water.

"Here, Molly, take it," she insists, pushing it toward me.

I swallow it without question, washing it down with a sip of tepid water.

"Where did you get this?" I ask. My parents keep all the medication under lock and key. If they're not home, I have to wait for them.

"They gave me one," she says. "For emergencies."

If you threaten suicide, your parents will give your migraine medication to your thirteen-year-old sister.

"Is it over?" I ask.

"It was the brother," Hazel says, "the whole time."

"Huh."

"Are you tired? Do you want to watch another? They're doing a marathon."

"I think I'm tired. My head hurts. I'm going to lie down."

Hazel follows me upstairs. I wash my face and brush my teeth. I'm already wearing pajamas; I don't remember putting them on.

In my room, Hazel sits on the edge of the bed. I crawl around her and she pulls the covers over me, like a smaller, younger version of our mother. She gets up and pulls the blinds shut and then she turns my light off and sits back down next to me.

"Feel better?"

"Yeah," I say. "Getting better."

She is as quiet as a cat. Her breathing is completely inaudible.

She twines one of her fingers around one of my fingers, and I squeeze weakly. This is code for something. We've never talked about it and we don't know what it means but it's a code. I move over on the bed and she lies down next to me and curls up with her nose just pressing into my neck. I can feel the pulse in my neck magnified by the pressure of Hazel's nose and I have such a strong sense of déjà vu. It comes from nowhere. Hazel with her nose against my neck. It feels so specific.

"What's wrong with her?" Clancy says from the doorway.

"She has a headache," Hazel says.

"I have a pill. Do you need a pill, Molly?"

When you threaten suicide, your parents will also entrust your migraine medication to your younger brother.

"I gave her mine," Hazel says.

"Hey—who was it? The creepy friend?" Clancy asks.

"The brother," Hazel says.

"The brother?"

"I didn't see it coming," she says.

"I'll be downstairs. Call me if you need anything."

He closes the door.

Hazel rolls over onto her back. We stare up at the ceiling together. It's too dark to see anything but our shoulders touch and I can tell her eyes are open.

"Did I know?" I ask her.

"Know what?" she says.

"Did I think it was the brother?" Usually I'm good at guessing.

"Oh," she says, laughing. "Yes. Yes, you knew it was the brother. Should have listened to you."

"Nailed it," I say. Hazel laughs more. She finds my hand

underneath the blanket and squeezes it.

"Molly," she says, "I'm so happy you're here."

"You're so weird," I answer.

When I wake up in the middle of the night, she is gone.

TEN.

I wake up late the next morning. Someone has turned my alarm off, left me a glass of water on my bedside table with another small pill beside it. There's a yellow mixing bowl on the carpet next to the bed. I'm glad I didn't need to use it.

I look at the clock. Halfway through second period.

My head feels normal again, so I skip the pill and pull myself out of bed. I could get away with going back to sleep, but I'm supposed to meet Sayer later. My parents won't let me out of the house if I don't go to school.

I shower. My mother's left a note on the counter downstairs. Text her if I need anything. Let her know if I decide to stay home or go to school. She's left my car keys next to the note. I have a bowl of cereal and grab a jacket. I can tell it's cold outside. There's a breeze and the sky is blue and the clouds are moving fast.

My backpack is by the door and I find myself hoping that sometime during the hours I can't remember, I managed to do some homework.

Not that it matters now.

My teachers are used to half-completed assignments from me.

They sort of accept it, at this point.

I used to be at the top of my class. Sophomore year into the beginning of junior, I was a straight-A student.

And then I sort of lost it.

In the car, I keep the radio down. I check my phone at a stop sign, finding messages from Erie, from Hazel and my mom, and one from Sayer.

From Sayer.

My heart does some weird skipping motion in my chest and I toss the phone back on the passenger seat, continue through the intersection after what I'm sure is an abnormally long stop.

I didn't even read it. I'm sure the only reason he would have texted me so early is to cancel whatever tentative plans we had. Now, of course, I'm wondering if we even had plans. Did I make the entire thing up? That seems like something I might do.

But it happened, right?

I know it happened.

It must have happened.

I don't look at my phone again until I'm parked in the school lot.

The text from Erie asks me where the hell I am. From my mom and Hazel, it's concern.

From Sayer . . .

It's a promise to pick me up at four.

We'll go for a drive, he says.

Have dinner, if I want to.

His number, finally, so I can put him in my contacts list. So he won't show up as private anymore.

My heart beats a steady staccato against my chest as I gather up my things and walk to school. I go to the principal's office, let them know I'm here, and instead of being upset, the secretary seems practically overjoyed to see me.

"Ms. Pierce," she croons in her heavy, syrupy voice. I can never remember her name. "Your mother called. Told me you might not make it at all. I'm so happy to see you're feeling better."

Yes.

That's me.

Feeling Better: The Story of Molly Pierce.

I laugh at my own joke. (It's an old one between Clancy and me: thinking up titles for our future autobiographies.) The secretary beams, clearly thinking she's delighted me.

That's me, too.

Delighted.

"Guess I'll just go, then," I say, ducking out the door, "to class, you know."

She waves me off and I make my way to my locker. I text my mom, let her know I'm here. I text Hazel. Tell her I'm fine. I text Erie, even though I'll see her soon.

It takes me a minute to remember what day it is, to figure out what class falls when in our six-day rotational schedule. I've missed the first ten minutes of Spanish, and I walk there as quickly as I can.

Luckily my Spanish teacher seems not to care much about my tardiness, as I've just realized the nameless secretary forgot to give me a note excusing my considerable lateness.

I slide into my usual seat next to Erie. Back row. She stares at me.

Luka isn't in this class. He took French.

I take a long time getting my book out, pulling my notebook from my bag, finding the right pen. Erie never takes her eyes off me.

She rips a piece of paper from her notebook, scribbles something on it, tosses it boldly on my desk.

The Spanish teacher is a hundred years old and is always forgetting where she left her glasses.

Where the hell were you? her note demands.

Overslept. Migraine. I texted you.

I toss the note back and she seems slightly mollified by this answer. She doesn't grab her phone to check, which is nice. We go back and forth like this for most of the class.

Still meeting Sayer today?

Four o'clock.

Plans?

Drive around. Maybe dinner. He's picking me up.

She considers her response for a while; when I look at her, she's lost outside the window somewhere, chewing on her pen cap.

Finally, she writes something. Throws it at me.

Carbon's getting on my nerves.

Is that really his name, though? I mean—really?

It's his name.

Getting on your nerves how?

Like, making up poems about me. Leaving them in my locker.

That sounds sweet.

He wrote a sestina about my hair.

How does one even do that?

Every word—you know, every repeating word—it was just "hair."

That's not how you write a sestina.

That's what I said.

Huh.

I actually write that. I write *huh* and then I throw the note back at her, and it's almost the end of the period and she doesn't respond. She crumples up the paper and tosses it into her backpack.

"Luka's asked out three girls so far," Erie says a few minutes later. We're at her locker. She's digging for a piece of gum. "At least—that's what he says."

"Three girls before lunch. Impressive."

"They all said no."

"That's not true," Luka says, materializing behind us. "One of them said *definitely* no. The others were gentler. Sort of like—*well, no, not at this venture.*"

"Not at this venture?" Erie says.

"Slightly less impressive," I revise.

"Yeah, well. This is your fault," Luka says, shrugging.

"I heard girls like when you write them sestinas," I say. "Try that."

"What's a sestina?" Luka asks.

Erie emerges from her locker with a single piece of gum. After some deliberation, she tears it into three pieces and hands them over.

"I do have nice hair," she says.

"I've never noticed," Luka says. He takes the gum and pushes past us.

Erie is momentarily stunned, so I shut her locker for her and take her arm and lead her down the hall after him.

"Do you think he—"

"No, Erie, I do not think he meant it," I say.

"Well, why do you think he—"

"I don't know—because he's Luka."

"But he didn't have to—"

"Oh, look," I say, pointing. "Carbon."

We all have study hall together next, and although Luka was ahead of us, he somehow manages to get there five minutes late. He plants himself next to me. Erie and Carbon have left a seat empty on my other side. They're whispering about something.

"What about her hair?" Luka whispers loudly, prompting an irritated look from Mr. Stone, who's monitoring what is supposed to be our silent study hall.

"Shh," I say.

Luka shrugs and settles back into his seat. He takes out a book and proceeds to not read it.

"What do you think about it, though?" he asks, nudging my side with his elbow and pointing over to where Erie and Carbon are sitting.

"What about it?"

"I give it, what—a week? Another week?"

"I don't know."

"Well, what do you think about him?"

"I don't know."

"And do you even think that's his real name?"

"I don't know."

"Hey, you're getting really great at conversations. Been practicing?"

"Sorry, I just—is it a little hot in here? I feel sort of hot."

I feel weird. It's like the auditorium is falling out of focus, like my eyes aren't working properly.

"I'm not hot," Luka says. "Still seeing Sayer tonight?"

"Yup."

"Plans?"

"Dunno. He said we'd drive around."

"Sounds fun." A pause. "He just seems a little weird, right? A little off?"

"He's not off, Jesus—Luka, his brother just died."

"What? He has a brother?"

"What?"

"What? Oh, are you talking about . . . No, I was talking about him. Carbon. I mean, it can't be his name—right? It's not his name."

"Carbon? What? I don't know. Why do you even—"

"It's just, you know, it's not even a *real* name. It's an element. Is it an element? Is carbon an element?"

"I don't know, I think it's a chemical."

"Right, a chemical element. And not a name."

"Whatever, what do you care?"

"I don't," he says. "Hey, do you want some water? I'm going to the bathroom. I'll get you some water. You look a little weird. Do you feel weird?"

"I just feel hot," I say.

Hot and blurry. Hot and indistinct, like the edges of my eyeballs are wiggling and causing the room to warp out of sync.

"Water will help," Luka says, using my shoulder to heave himself up. "I'll get you some water."

I try and mumble thanks but Luka has vanished and I am somewhere I don't recognize.

I'm with Sayer.

It's weeks ago.

I remember.

I know Sayer.

I'm with Sayer and he leans in and kisses me and I kiss him back.

And then he tells me he loves me and I tell him I love him back.

Sayer.

He lied to me.

I know him.

ELEVEN.

I burst out of study hall and slam directly into someone. I try and push past them but they've grabbed my wrist, gently but firmly, and I look up at their face hoping it's . . . I don't know. Hoping it's my brother, I guess. He's the only person who will leave me alone, no questions, if I ask him to.

It's Bret.

I feel my heart plummet to somewhere around my stomach. Of course it's Bret. Isn't it always? Every embarrassing, awful thing that happens to me, and there's Bret Jennings. It's like he's attracted to my awkward moments.

"Molly, whoa," he says. "You okay?"

"What, sure! Of course! Bathroom! Going to the. You know."

There's no time to rethink the order of those words. I've already said them.

"You look a little pale," he says.

"Hot," I blurt out. "I mean, I'm a little hot. It's hot. I'm fine."

"I didn't see you in first period."

That catches my interest, I can't lie. Bret noticed I wasn't in first period? But then I remember: I'm his lab partner. Biology was first period today. I left him by himself.

"I know, I'm sorry. I hope I didn't miss anything important. I mean, I hope you didn't need me or anything."

"You're always needed," he says, and it's like he says it before he realizes how awkward it will sound. It falls to the floor, heavy, and Bret blushes and squeezes my elbow quickly, walks away even quicker.

The squeeze of the elbow means a lot of things.

Please pretend I didn't say that.

Please pretend I didn't mean that.

Please pretend I didn't say that but also know that at least on some subconscious level I meant it.

I don't have time to dwell on that further. I barely make it to the bathroom before the memory comes back, full force this time. I lock myself in a stall and let it hit me. I don't think I have a choice.

• • •

"But what will he say?" I ask, my mouth turning downward in a flirty, unfamiliar pout.

We're in a coffeehouse, a dark place with a small, raised platform, a stool, and a microphone. A boy with a guitar has just finished a song. The few people who are listening clap hard. Sayer and I join them; I even cup my hands around my mouth and holler my appreciation.

It's Parker up there. Sayer's best friend. He finds us in the crowd and gives a half wave, a goofy smile, launches right into the next song. It's one of my favorites. "I'm Leaving you, Louella."

I asked once who Louella was.

He said she was no one. He made her up.

But it feels like she's real. Like maybe he just changed her name.

Sayer gets my attention again, grabs my knee under the table. I laugh, ticklish, and push him off. Hold his hand instead. Turn serious. Look at him.

"It doesn't matter," he says.

"Of course it matters," I say. "He's your brother."

"He's an idiot."

"Maybe. Still your brother."

"He'll understand."

We both know he won't understand. We both know Lyle feels like he deserves me. Like I owe him something.

I didn't ask for his help.

But on the other hand—

I don't want him sad. I don't want him hurt.

He's my friend. My best friend, really. He means everything to me and the last thing I want to do is hurt him.

But I don't think I can help it.

"Hey," Sayer says. "Hey."

I shrug. I'm afraid that if I say anything, I'll start to cry.

"I have to go soon," I say.

He nods. "I know. Just don't worry about Lyle. I'll talk to him."

"No. I want to. Let me. I think it should come from me."

Sayer nods.

I have to go. I try and stand up, but he's too quick for me. He leans across the table. He kisses me and I kiss him back. It's just Sayer and me and this music and this tiny coffeehouse and nothing else.

"Don't leave," he says. And something in the way he says it, it's more than that. It means something more.

"You know I have to."

"You could stay."

"You know I can't stay."

"Who knows. Maybe you'd like me."

"I know I would."

Another kiss.

"I love you," he says.

It's the first time he's said it.

I feel some kind of warmth spread through my body.

A fleeting burst of happiness mixed with a stubborn, permanent sadness that I can never completely get away from.

"I love you, too."

In the bathroom, I am not crying. I am not crying because I refuse to cry, because I have balled up my fists and shoved them into my eyes until angry white spots dance across my vision. Only then do I leave the stall, wipe off my smudged eye makeup with a stiff paper towel, check the side of my neck for the pulse I am never entirely positive I will find.

I want to call Alex again but I don't. There's no point. He knows what's happening to me and he won't tell me. He tried to tell me before, maybe, but never hard enough.

I take my cell phone out of my book bag and fight the sudden, wild urge to drown it in water.

Who could I possibly use it to call?

Everyone I know has lied to me.

My friends, they know. My family—Hazel sitting on my car, putting her nose against my neck. Sayer. Everyone knows except me and I hate them for it.

Only one person has escaped my anger and suddenly I want to see him. I need to talk to him.

I need to talk to my brother.

And somehow I know I get away with too much.

The nurse, she basically lets me come and go as I please. My teachers don't even question my frequent absences and lateness. I have no idea where my brother is right now, but the school secretary will tell me. I don't know how I know she'll tell me but I'm out of the bathroom and practically running to the main office, and when I get there she doesn't even ask me any questions. She actually calls the classroom herself and talks to the teacher and tells him to send my brother here.

What the fuck is wrong with me?

Something terrible, apparently, if I can get away with all this.

I see him coming, confused, thinking he's probably in trouble. I shout a quick thanks to the nameless secretary, dart out of the office, grab his arm, and drag him down the hallway toward the door that will lead us away. Outside.

He doesn't struggle. So he knows.

Only outside does he question me.

"Where are we going?" he says. "Not that I'm not grateful, you know, for getting me out of algebra."

I don't answer him until we're far enough away from the school that I don't feel like its walls are crushing me anymore. Then I turn on him. We're on the path leading to the student parking lot; it's shaded on either side by thick rows of trees. We're in the dead middle; we can't see the school or the cars. Perfectly hidden from view.

"Clancy, you have to be honest. Okay? All questions. Honest."

He only thinks about it for a minute, but it's long enough so that I know he's telling the truth when he shrugs and says okay.

"What's happening to me?"

"Be more specific," he says, sighing and looking around me, squirming a little like he's afraid of something.

"What do you—"

"Yes or no questions. Ask me yes or no questions. And do it quickly, because, you know. You could check out any minute."

Yes or no? How can I possibly find anything out by asking only yes or no questions? I spin away from him, spin back. Try to counteract the spinning going on inside my head with my physical motion. Try to correct my balance.

Okay, Molly. Relax. Think.

"Something is wrong with me, right? And everybody knows except me."

"Yes."

"Everybody knows about my memory loss? My blackouts?"

It feels weird saying it aloud.

"Yup."

"And they know why it's happening?"

"Yup."

"And they're supposed to act like they don't?"

"Yes."

Fuck.

Okay, relax.

Relax.

God, what else. What else? This is the hardest thing in the world.

"Am I . . . fuck, Clancy, am I fucking crazy? I feel crazy."

He smirks.

He actually smirks, the asshole, but he recovers quickly and he shrugs and he holds out his hand, palm down, and rocks it back and forth.

Sort of.

I'm sort of crazy.

Great.

"So what am I supposed to do?" I say. Quieter this time.

And his face clouds over. Just a moment it's there: a shadow. And then he shrugs again, runs a hand through his messy hair.

"You should talk to Sayer. I'm sure he'll have plenty to say about it."

TWELVE.

How can I go back to school?

But I do.

I go back and I sit through the rest of my classes.

Erie tries to talk to me but I brush her off as gently as I can manage. I smile and hope maybe she'll think everything is okay. But Erie. She knows. What she knows, I can't guess, but she knows. And so I imagine she isn't fooled by a simple smile.

A hundred times I want to get up and leave but I don't. A hundred times I think about calling Sayer, canceling our plans, but I don't. A hundred times I want to find my brother again, drag him outside, make him look me in the eyes and use his gaze like an anchor. Use him like a life-boat, use him like a parachute.

But I don't.

He told me to talk to Sayer and so I will.

I tell myself my anger will abate as the day goes by, but if anything I am angrier than ever when the last bell rings.

Clancy is waiting by my locker. He puts his arm around my shoulders when we walk to my car and nobody says anything. Shouldn't people say something? Make fun of him? Shout insults at this sudden break in his usually stoic demeanor?

But they don't. They won't.

For some reason, they wouldn't do that to me.

And, by association, they wouldn't do that to him.

In some weird way, he might be lucky to be my brother.

"Why the yes or no?" I ask when we get to the middle school. I don't know if he'll answer me but we have time to wait for Hazel, anyway, and it fills the silence.

"Alex said it might be easier for you," he says.

"Why?"

"No idea," he says.

"You all talk to Alex?"

"Not, like, daily, Molly, so don't get all weird. Just sometimes."

My nail polish is blue. It's chipping. It's light blue and it's chipping. I look at it for a long time, and Clancy looks at me for a long time and then he looks away. And after that Hazel gets in the car and I try shifting to drive before I remember the engine is off. And then I try shifting into drive again before I remember the engine is still off and then I finally turn the engine on and when the motor comes to life, I press my forehead against the steering wheel and take a deep breath.

"Molly?" Hazel says from the backseat.

"I'm fine," I say automatically.

"Clancy?" she says.

"She's fine, Hazel."

Hazel looks at me in the rearview. I try not to meet her gaze but it's hard. Her blue eyes fill up the whole mirror.

They're both doing shifts at the bookstore today, so I drop them off first, and I drive home in silence, the radio turned off and the windows rolled up and only the soft breeze of heat from the vents to disturb my forced peace.

I don't really have time for a nap before Sayer gets here, but I lie down anyway. It takes me a long time to get to sleep and my alarm goes off practically the second I do and I end up feeling more tired than when I got home. But at least the circles under my eyes have faded a little.

A very little.

When I pull myself out of bed, it's ten of four and I shower in three minutes, get dressed in another three.

With four minutes to go, I sit on the edge of my bed and wonder what the fuck is going on.

I've been wondering that a lot.

With each new memory that surfaces, my grip on things gets a little more slippery.

A little farther away.

What do I know so far?

The basics, Molly. Just think about the basics. Like Clancy's yes or no questions, it might be the easiest way to organize things.

Okay.

The basics.

I was friends with Lyle. He told me how he felt about me. I told him that I couldn't return the feelings because I had feelings for someone else.

For his brother, apparently.

But there's something between us, Lyle and me. Something that happened to me or something he did for me. Something that makes him feel like I owe it to him.

I have no idea what that could be.

The doorbell.

The journey down the stairs seems to take forever, and with each step my anger boils up under my skin until I swear I have turned red with the heat of it.

And when I open the door, I know Sayer can tell, because at first he smiles and he opens his mouth to say hello and then he shuts it and takes one tiny step backward. More like a shuffle. He shuffles backward and I step out of the house and plant myself firmly on the welcome mat and I cross my arms over my chest because suddenly it is freezing.

"I told you I would explain," he says.

"You lied to me."

"I can explain now."

"But you lied to me."

"What did you remember?" he says.

"No, wait," he says.

"Can we just . . . can we get out of here?" he says.

"Let me get my coat."

A half an hour later and Sayer has pulled the car to the side of the road and we're walking through a brief patch of forest to where, I know, the trees will open up on to a public beach. It's sure to be deserted with how cold it is and with the sun already so close to setting. The perfect place to talk.

He drags a blanket from the trunk of his car, so I guess he planned this. Or, I don't know, maybe the blanket came with the car. Or maybe he bought the blanket for the car and now he just keeps it in the trunk so in case he breaks down somewhere in the middle of a snowstorm he can use it to keep from freezing to death.

He spreads the blanket on the sand and I sit on it without accepting his tentative offer of help.

And then I start talking before he's even settled himself. Because if I don't just jump right into it, I may never start.

"I remembered the warehouse, with Lyle, and I remembered the time before that. We were in a graveyard. The graveyard in town, next to the beach."

"And then?" He seems to know there's something else.

"I remembered us at a coffeehouse. We were watching your friend play guitar. Parker. He played a song I liked. He waved to us. You told me not to worry about what Lyle thought and then I said I'd tell him about us. Then you kissed me and you told me you loved me. I think it was the first time you said it. And then I left. I said I had to go and it felt like it was really important. That I had to leave immediately or something bad would happen."

"The warehouse," Sayer says. He's staring straight ahead at the water. "The warehouse and then the graveyard and then Parker's show. And that's how you remembered them? That's the order?"

"Yes. You said you'd never met me before."

And then—

"The hospital," I say.

I feel sick to my stomach. A feeling I'm getting used to.

"At the hospital, when I called you from Lyle's phone. You said my name. I knew you said my name."

I realize it's been a week exactly. A week since Lyle died. A week since I watched Lyle die.

"I'm sorry," he breathes. "I didn't want to upset you."

I don't know what else to say so I wrap my arms around my legs and hug my knees to my chest and put my chin between them.

"Why is the order important?" I mumble.

"It's backward," he says. He looks at me like he wants to comfort me, put his arm around me, but he doesn't.

I don't want him to, but I do want him to. I am somewhere equidistant between not wanting him to and wanting him to.

"What do you mean?"

"You're remembering everything backward. The last time you saw Lyle, right before the accident, was in the warehouse. The time before that was by the graveyard. When you told him about us. That last time you saw me was right before that—"

"When you told me you loved me and I told you I'd tell Lyle," I interrupt.

"Yeah," he says.

More facts, Molly.

You have more facts.

There's a series of memories, right? All the times from my blackouts that I didn't remember before. And it seems like they all have to do with Lyle and Sayer and my relationship with the two of them.

And I don't remember the moments, aside from the warehouse and the graveyard and the coffeehouse. I can't remember any of them.

But somehow, when I blacked out . . .

When I was in them.

I remembered everything.

Like a two-way mirror.

Like a one-way street.

Like a—

Stop, Molly.

Breathe, Molly.

"Molly?" Sayer says.

I look at him. Startled.

"I'm sorry," he says. "I'm sorry I lied to you."

"Did you have to?" I ask.

I don't know where that came from.

I was about to say something awful. I was about to yell at him.

I've never really been good at sticking to my guns.

He seems relieved. He seems sort of grateful.

And he seems like he means it.

When he says, "Yes. I did."

THIRTEEN.

You take it for granted. Waking up. Going to school, talking to your friends. Watching a show on television or reading a book or going out to lunch.

You take for granted going to sleep at night, getting up the next day, and remembering everything that happened to you before you closed your eyes.

We take it for granted.

We forget stuff along the way, sure, but mostly it's little stuff. We forget where we put our keys or we forget to turn the curling iron off or we lie awake in bed in the middle of the night, convinced we left the stove on. Convinced we left the front door unlocked. Convinced we forgot to set the alarm.

And as we grow up, we accept that our memory gets worse. Sometimes we can't remember what day it is. Sometimes we can't remember if we washed our hair already. We stand in the shower dripping, unmoving.

We forget to put deodorant on.

We forget our sunglasses on the kitchen counter.

We run out of the house without our car keys. Without our purse.

Older still and now other things start to go. We cannot remember our children's names. We call them every name we can think of until we get to the right one. We know we're right because they finally answer us.

We put our blouse on backward.

Maybe we wear two different socks. Two different shoes.

We get into the car and we forget where we're going, or we remember where we're going but we forget how to get there.

And then one day maybe we forget everything altogether. We forget how old we are and we forget our names and we forget when to eat and when to sleep and we lose weight and we get big circles under our eyes.

This kind of forgetting, this is almost okay.

Because it is expected.

But when you are young, when you are my age, you take it for granted.

You get up. You have your day. You go to sleep.

You remember everything you did.

This is normal.

We remember.

We live and we remember.

You live and you remember.

But me.

Me, I live and I forget.

Except now.

Now I am remembering.

And I'm not sure what I liked better.

Being in the dark or being thrust—without warning—into the light.

Lyle tells me how he feels about me. It is early fall. September. I knew this was coming.

I knew this was coming, but it is still a surprise when the words leave his mouth. He brings to me a small Mexican restaurant. It's out of the way and a little run-down, and from the outside it looks like some kind of trap. There is no one else there. I get quesadillas. I sip water the entire time he talks to me, and when he's finished, I can't even meet his eyes.

What is worse, to have your heart broken or to be the one doing the breaking?

I'll take the first choice, any day.

I'm good at being unhappy.

I'm good at accommodating my sadness.

I can't be with Lyle.

I can't be with anybody, really, but I've made an exception for Sayer. Why? I have no idea. Because I like the way he looks at me, I guess. I like the way he smells. I like his hands, his fingers. I like the way he talks. I think he is the first person who has ever known me. The real me. Not the Molly everyone is accustomed to, but the other me who lives deep inside her. He's the only person who's ever seen me before.

"Is it because of everything that happened?" he says.

I shake my head. "No, Lyle, it has nothing to do with that."

"Is there someone else?"

Yes, there's someone else.

I love your brother. I love Sayer. I think he'll tell me soon. Maybe in a dark coffeehouse while someone is playing the guitar he will tell me and I'll be able to stick around long enough to tell him back.

"Don't be weird," I say. "There's nobody else."

"Not some guy at school?"

"Not some guy at school."

"Not Luka?"

"That's not funny."

"So it's nobody. It's just not me."

"You know it's complicated. You know I love you."

"Sure, I know you love me. Sure."

"I'm not exactly in a place to . . ."

What?

I'm not exactly in a place to what?

To commit myself to anyone.

To be committed, maybe. To a mental institution. To an insane asylum.

But not to a person.

Even with Sayer, I know it's impossible. It's an impossible situation I let spin out of control. It's not fair to him and it's not fair to me, but for now it is warm and it is nice and I think about him all the time.

When I can think about anything, I think about him.

I finish my water. I shake the cup and sip from the straw, get only air and bubbles.

"You know how much I care about you," Lyle says. "Right? You know I would do anything for you."

"Yeah," I say. Weak, I know, but I can't think of anything else.

Yeah, I know you would do anything for me, Lyle. You already have.

And maybe that's the problem. Maybe I don't like feeling, on some weird level, that I am always in your debt.

That you consider me to be always in your debt.

How can someone live with that hanging over her? How could you expect two people to have a successful relationship with that always in between them? Hogging the bed. Backing up the drain in the shower. Leaving the lights on.

"That's it, then?" he asks.

I maybe nod. I try and nod, but I'm not sure if my neck obeys my command.

"It's okay," he says. He's even smiling a little. "I have time."

Everything is about you, isn't it, Lyle? You have time or you don't. You love me or you don't. I owe you something. You are owed.

I guess I roll my eyes, because he asks me why I rolled my eyes.

"I don't know, Lyle. Maybe I have something in them."

"You're upset?"

"No. I'm fine."

I flag down the waiter. He takes our empty plates and leaves the check on the edge of the table.

"How are you possibly upset?" Lyle asks. "You're not the one who—"

"I'm never the one, am I?" I ask.

"You're always the one! Didn't I just—"

"Never mind. Please, just forget it."

I pick up the check. I show it to him. We split it.

"I'll never get you," he says in the parking lot. He shakes his head.

Of course you won't. It is impossible to get me. Because you could never understand how it is to be fleeting. To be momentary. To be detached and to be alone and to be always dependent on somebody else.

To be transitory and to be ephemeral.

"Come on," I say, grabbing his hand. "I don't know how much time I have left."

Alex waits until I open my eyes. His office seems overexposed and blurry, and he is just a bright shadow against a brighter, indistinct landscape.

Wednesday. More pieces fall into place. More memories come into focus.

Something has developed between yesterday and today: this weird feeling that I am not watching myself but a copy of myself. Some of the things I say, I would never say in real life. The Molly in my memories, she is bolder than I am. She is less inhibited. She is prettier. She does her makeup better than I do. Her hair. She holds her shoulders differently and she always smiles like she knows what everyone is thinking.

I never know what anyone is thinking.

As soon as my eyes have adjusted to the light, I tell Alex about this fresh memory and we talk about *what I think it means* and *how it makes me feel.*

Gone is my insistence that he tells me what happened to me.

Gone is my anger toward everyone I know.

Gone is my indignation that they have kept me in the dark.

Because I think it makes sense, what Alex told me. I

think I have to figure it out for myself.

I talk for an hour, and at the end of the hour I feel better than I have in one week and one day. Since I pulled Lyle's helmet off and ruined my favorite gray sweater.

One week. A lot has happened in one week.

When I leave Alex's office, I find Clancy in my car, listening to the radio with his eyes closed. He must have taken the spare set of car keys from my parents.

"Hey," I say, sliding into the driver's seat.

"Drive me to the bookstore?" he says. He's wearing his signature uniform. Black jeans, black band T-shirt, black zip-up hoodie.

My brother. The only one I don't have to pretend around anymore. Everyone else thinks I'm blissfully ignorant.

"How did you get here?"

"Walked," he says.

"I thought it was Hazel and me tonight."

"We switched," he explains. "She has some book report to finish."

I pull into traffic. Every time I pull into traffic now, I have to stop myself from looking in my rearview mirror. Searching for the boy on the motorcycle.

"How's Alex?" Clancy says.

"I'm not going to talk about my therapy session with you," I reply immediately.

"Well, how was Sayer yesterday?"

"I'm also not going to talk about Sayer with you."

"What would you like to talk about, Molly?"

"Nothing. I don't really want to talk about anything."

"Cool. So next time you pull me out of my class, I won't want to talk about anything either," he says.

"Look, I'm sorry," I say, backpedaling.

I really am sorry. And I meant what I said: I'm not angry anymore.

But that doesn't mean I particularly embrace talking about everything.

"Alex was fine. I remembered some more stuff and I talked to him about it. He said he's happy with my progress."

Clancy laughs, a sharp, abrupt laugh that makes me jump a mile. My eyes shoot to the rearview mirror, shoot back.

"What was that for?" I ask.

"He actually said that? 'I'm happy with your progress, Molly'? I didn't think shrinks said shit like that."

He's beside himself. Giggling, my brother.

"They don't call them shrinks anymore," I mumble.

"And Sayer?" he says, when he gets a handle on himself.

"It was okay. We're in love, I guess. Only I don't remember any of it."

"Must be weird."

"Yeah. Hey, Clancy—what happens? When I black out, what am I like?"

He takes a deep breath. "At first, I couldn't even tell. It

was always Hazel. She knew even before . . ."

"Before what?"

"Before anyone," he says. "But then, you know. It got easier. Over the years."

"The years? But it's only been happening—"

"The past year, whatever. I'm not a calendar," he says dismissively. "Most of the time, yeah, I can tell. Even though you act basically the same. You're not that different. Just little things."

"The way I hold my shoulders."

"The way you hold your shoulders, yeah. It makes you taller."

There's a long silence. We get to the bookstore and I park around the back. My parents are here; their minivan is taking up almost two spots. My dad must have parked it.

I turn the engine off.

Clancy makes a move to open the door, but I grab the sleeve of his sweatshirt.

"Wait," I say.

He waits.

I wait.

We wait.

"It's like everything is spreading out in front of me," I say.

I expect him to roll his eyes. Snort. Something. But to his credit, he manages only a small smile.

"What do you mean?"

"Like before, it was just black. I would look back over the past year and there would be these huge, gaping holes. But now it's like I almost have a choice. Like I can keep going back and back and peel off layers until I reach the very beginning. It's like it's up to me. I don't have to remember, if I don't want to. Today, with Alex, I made that happen. I made myself remember. I was given a choice, and I made the choice to remember."

A hand through his hair and a heavy sigh that could mean a million things or nothing at all.

Then: "Yeah, I guess that makes sense," he says.

"Really?"

"With everything I know about you, yeah. That makes sense."

With everything he knows about me.

He gets out of the car.

Everything he knows about me, I don't even know about myself.

FOURTEEN.

I can let the memories in whenever I want.

At the bookstore Clancy takes the register, tidies up the front of the store, dusts the shelves, and throws open the windows to let in the brisk October air. My parents leave at six and I bury myself in the back room, pulling books out of cardboard boxes and entering titles and ISBNs into the computer.

This is my favorite room in the store and it might be my favorite room on the planet. Here, the carpet is thick and you can sit on the floor and surround yourself in the smell of old classics. Mystery novels, my father's favorite. The memoirs my mother reads on Saturday mornings, refusing to leave her bedroom before noon. Drinking cup after cup of coffee that Hazel brings to her. Just cream. Lots of cream but no sugar.

Here, I can take my time. Clancy will leave me alone. Not even the occasional chime of the bell on the front door disturbs me. My father installed it himself to announce the arrival of each new customer. It's only background noise. Everything fades away. I can close my eyes and let the images rush back to me. See myself doing things I can't remember doing. Saying things I can't remember saying.

I fall in love with Sayer.

Or, I remember falling in love with Sayer.

It's hard to sort out the present and the past when you're inviting everything in at once.

What is it like?

It's like a movie screen.

I close my eyes and watch everything happen, and once it's done, it's done. It sinks into the background and it behaves just like a regular memory. It's faded, just like a regular memory. You can never recall the exact colors. The exact smells. You can think about it, but it never replays from beginning to end.

But once it's there, it's there.

And it's been so long since I've remembered things so clearly, at first I don't know what to do with myself.

At first, I am so overjoyed I could cry.

But I don't cry.

You learn not to cry when you've been labeled suicidal.

Would I have actually tried to kill myself? What if Hazel never overheard my threat or what if I never said it in the first place? If I never got help?

I think about that all the time.

And I have no idea.

And to say that.

To say I don't know if I would have done it. Killed myself.

Not knowing—that's a fucking awful feeling.

This is the next thing I remember.

We're in Sayer's apartment.

It's a studio in a big old Victorian house his landlord converted. It's small but it's nice. The paint is peeling off the walls in some spots and the door to the bathroom doesn't shut all the way and you have to light the stove with a match because the pilot's constantly going out, but it's a home. It's Sayer's home and I guess that makes it sort of like my home, too.

Sayer, he's good with things. He always has his ladder out and he keeps his tools spread over the kitchen table. He works at night when he can't sleep. He can hardly ever sleep. He fixes the drip in the bathroom sink. He changes the wiring in the ceiling fan so it turns on and off from a switch.

I like to watch him work because it's foreign to me.

If something breaks, my parents call a repairman. Clancy barely knows how to change a lightbulb and Hazel tends not to notice. She could spend an entire week bathing in ice-cold water, the thought never crossing her mind that something must be wrong with the heater.

Sayer's been fixing up the apartment one area at a time in return for breaks on his rent. His landlord, Jackie, loves him because he's polite and he's never loud and he keeps everything clean. He's even helped out with other apartments in the building. If the landlord gets a call and he can't make it right away, he'll see if Sayer can go over. Some months he works so much he doesn't have to pay any rent at all.

"Forget it," Jackie said one day. "Forget it, kid, I'm not taking a check from you. After all the work you've done."

That night we went out to dinner, to the fanciest restaurant in town (which, truth be told, isn't all that fancy). But I wore a dress and Sayer wore khakis and a brown tweed sports jacket and it was nice.

In those moments, I felt like I had my own life.

It was a secret life. I kept it secret from my parents and I kept it secret from Luka and Erie and from Hazel and Clancy. I kept it secret from Lyle.

It wasn't their business. It wasn't anybody's business. It was only mine.

Could I have just this one thing to myself?

I knew I'd have to let it go eventually.

But for now. I thought I loved him.

I did love him.

I loved Sayer.

I loved his apartment and I loved his hands and I loved every memory I had of him.

And that's why I kept them so secret. Secret even from myself.

It's windy. The windows in Sayer's apartment are old and they rattle in their frames and the wind keeps up a low, constant whistle. I'm supposed to see Lyle today. He wants to take me to a Mexican restaurant. He says it's the best Mexican food I'll ever have.

Sayer is scraping old paint from a doorframe. I'm on the couch, writing in a spiral-bound notebook. I keep these journals here; I keep this entire life here, locked safely in Sayer's linen closet. Pulled out only when I want to. Only when I can slip away.

"Water?" he says. He's off the ladder, in the kitchen. I must have been daydreaming.

"Sure, thanks."

He pours us each a glass and hands mine over with exaggerated flourish. "When are you meeting Lyle?"

"Soon."

"How long do you have?"

"A little longer than soon."

He laughs. Finishes his water and puts it on the coffee table. "Parker has a show next week."

"Where?"

"That coffeehouse I took you to. I'd like you to come."

"If I can. I want to."

"Try," he says.

"I'll try. You know I can't promise much."

"You can promise to try."

He touches a strand of my hair, pushes it away from my face.

"Of course I'll try. I promise I'll try."

"I wish I could see you more."

I wish I could see you more, too. I wish I could see you whenever I wanted. But you know I can't. I've told you why I can't. And I'm stupid for letting it get as far as it has, but now we're here and what am I supposed to do? What am I supposed to do?

He's very close to me. His breath on my cheek and my heart speeding up, beating irregularly. He's kissed me before, but it's still a shock. It's a shock every time it happens. This isn't supposed to happen to me! I'm not supposed to get this! I'm not supposed to be this happy.

His hands in my hair and his lips on my lips.

He can hear my heart. He has to be able to hear my heart. It's the loudest, most awkward heart in the world.

Books and carpet and cardboard boxes.

Pull yourself together, Molly.

You've kissed boys before. You kissed Sam Mandel and

that kid with the braces in seventh grade, whatever his name was. It was on a dare but you still kissed him. You kissed Zach Brayson in freshman year and in sophomore year you kissed Dan Flowers. And you kissed Will and you kissed Alan.

But did any of them kiss you like Sayer kissed you? Did any of them close their eyes like that, tilt your head up with their finger underneath your chin? Did any of them pull away and look at you like that afterward? Like you've just made their whole fucking life somehow perfect.

The next time you see him, Molly, he tells you he loves you. Has anyone ever told you he loved you?

No. No, it's only Sayer. Sayer tilting my head up. Sayer kissing me. Sayer in a coffeehouse, telling me he loves me.

Well I think I loved you, too, Sayer. I must have. I heard myself say it.

And remembering something is what makes it real.

Isn't it?

I don't know. I'm probably not the best judge of that.

I look at my watch. It's almost eight and time to close up the shop. I get my phone out of my backpack and I have twelve texts from Erie, of course. A text from Hazel.

And a text from Sayer.

I open the phone and read it three times before I'm sure it's real.

> Molly. Are you busy tomorrow? I'm worried about you and I miss you.

I guess I do love him. I have to love him. The people we love get under our skin and crawl through our veins and find their way into our heart. They choke up our blood flow and mess up our breathing and tangle themselves through our bodies like wire. Like razors, like fire.

We remember them even when we don't remember them.

We try and forget, but it's pointless.

Even amnesia. Even comas and brain damage and traumatic shock.

Whatever makes us not remember, we still remember.

Our minds flounder like fish but our bodies . . .

Our bodies remember.

FIFTEEN.

I walked with Sayer through forests alive with the colors of fall. Blazing flashes of red and orange and all shades of green and brown. He found a patch of wildflowers and pulled a yellow one from the ground, tucked it behind my ear, and pretended we lived a million years in the past.

"Milady, the flower suits you," he said, bowing low and waving one arm.

I laughed and danced away from him, hid behind tree trunks, and covered my mouth so he wouldn't hear me breathing.

But he found me. He always found me.

He kissed me with my back pressed against an oak tree,

and the sound of squirrels chasing each other scared me nearly half to death. I was always scared of being caught. In the back of my mind I was scared that anyone who saw us would know.

You are not supposed to have this! You are not supposed to have him!

What are you doing with her! they'd say to him.

Don't you know? Don't you know who she is?

This is when I tell him.

I tell him in the forest.

I don't know how he'll take it. I'm so scared I think I'll throw up, but I know I have to tell him. I have to be honest with him. You're supposed to be honest with the people you love and I think I'm falling in love with him. I'm the stupidest girl in the world for letting it get this far, but what's there to do now? It's here. I'm here. We're here in this forest and he's put a yellow flower behind my ear and he's kissed me with my back against an oak tree.

He asks a lot of questions. When I tell him, he is quiet at first like he's trying to figure out if I'm lying. If I'm lying, Sayer, I have the worst sense of humor in the universe. We sit together on a fallen tree trunk and at one point I put my face in my hands because I don't know.

Because I'm ashamed, I guess.

But Sayer, he pulls my hands away from my face and he never lets go of them.

He says my name. My name. And he asks a hundred

questions. All about when it started, what it means. How I feel and how I break away and how I go back.

I tell him how I met Lyle and his face gets pale, and for a while he doesn't say anything and he looks up at the blue sky through green leaves and I can almost feel him slipping away and so I hold his hands even tighter to keep him here with me.

You can't leave me. You're mine and you have to stay here.

I did it all for you! I want to shout it at the trees, claw it into my skin. Tattoo it across my arms.

I did it all for you, Molly, and now look what I'm doing. I'm undoing everything.

"Are you okay now?" he says.

"I'm okay now. I'm getting help."

"I'm here for you," he says finally.

He's like Clancy. You know they're being honest because they don't rush anything. They consider their options. They'd tell you to fuck yourself, if that's what you needed to hear. But they would never promise you something they couldn't deliver.

After the forest we get grilled cheese sandwiches in a diner and Sayer finishes my fries.

I'm scared he'll never want to see me again, but even the possibility never leaves his lips. And I won't be the one to say it. I certainly won't be the one.

• • •

Things are omitted.

What I told Sayer in the forest, I can't guess. I know it shocked him and I know it terrified me to tell him, and I could hear my thoughts but they were only the thoughts that didn't give too much away.

So I'm still keeping secrets from myself, I guess.

I thought I had control over my memories, but as hard as I search for them I can't seem to grab on. It's like something keeps them just out of my reach. Like something inside me is holding them above my head. Locked them in a safe. Buried them in a mason jar in the middle of a field of wildflowers. Given me a spoon instead of a shovel. Wished me luck and sent me out in the middle of a pitch-black moonless night to dig. We're in Alaska and there's no sunlight for four months.

Good luck, Molly.

Here's hoping.

I text Sayer back and say

What about now? I'm free now.

I'm free now and I don't want to have to wait to see you.

Clancy and I close up the store; I drive him home and leave without going inside.

I know the way to Sayer's apartment. I remember the way to Sayer's apartment. I drive down winding seaside roads with the windows down, letting in the damp and chilly air. It's dark and nearing nine when I reach his driveway. There's a small parking area in back. I turn off the car and pick up my phone. I have three texts from my mother.

> **Where are you going?**
> **Are you aware it's a school night?**
> **Answer me!**

I call her.

Mom, I'm sorry. I'm sorry! There's just something I have to do. It's for school. It's a project. I completely forgot about it until Clancy mentioned something in the bookstore. Yeah, I know. I know I said I would try harder. I know, and that's why I'm taking care of it tonight. I'm perfectly safe. I'm doing some work at Erie's. I may stay over. Is it okay if I stay over?

When I get off the phone I text Erie.

> **If my mother calls, I'm sleeping over. School project.**

She responds within minutes.

> **Roger! Where are you really?**

I knew she'd want to know and if she's going to lie for me she might as well know why she's doing it.

> **I'm with Sayer.**

Her text comes almost immediately.

> **What! Wow! Two days in a row!**

> **Had to leave quickly yesterday.**

> **Well have fun! And be safe. And don't be**

late to school tomorrow. We have Pickney
first thing. You know how he is.

Roger.

I put my phone in my backpack and leave it in the car.

He's waiting for me by the back door and I throw myself into his arms. That feeling. The one where he is one side of a magnet and I am one side of another magnet and we are constantly reaching out to each other. It's stronger now.

I take him by surprise. He laughs at first and then he puts his arms around me. When I don't pull away, he says my name like a question. Like he's checking to see who I am.

"Molly?"

"Can I come inside?"

"Of course. Of course, yeah, come on."

On his couch he brings me water and I sit sipping it.

His apartment has changed. The amount of work he's done, it could almost be a completely different place.

"It looks great in here," I say.

I catch him by surprise, but he recovers and he sits down next to me. Our knees are almost touching.

"You remember?"

"It's easier now."

"That's good," he says.

Our bodies don't forget.

I feel the space between us like a charged bit of current.

Like a wave, like a vacuum. Like a hum. He's impossibly close but also unreachable, the distance from my knees to his knees is as wide as an ocean. He says something and I don't answer him. Or I answer him and I forget what I say. Or maybe I am the one who's said something and he's answered me or he hasn't. All I know is I feel like I'm falling into some unending ravine; and the pressure of falling so quickly is making my ears pop, it's making my stomach churn, it's making my eyes water. If I can't have him, I'll die. I'll hit the bottom and die. Something is telling me he's not mine, but without him I'll be stuck in the forest forever. A yellow flower in my hair and nothing to drink and no map to find my way out.

He says something again. This time he definitely says something, but I still don't hear what it is and somehow I've closed the gap between us and I've put my lips on his lips. Just for a minute I will be okay. Just for a minute this is what I need.

I try to tell him that, but it comes out like a moan and his hands on the small of my back are persistent. They are pressing. They are confident and they make me confident. They grip my shoulders and they ease me backward until he is on top of me on the couch.

Is this what I came over for?

Who knows? But it's what I want now.

Sayer's hips against my hips. Sayer's hands against the couch, pushing himself up so he won't crush me.

Sayer's mouth on my mouth and Sayer's lips and Sayer's teeth. And the way that Sayer tastes. And the beating of his heart against the beating of my heart.

Have I imagined what this might be like?

This back and forth motion, this up and down, this whirlwind, this heat.

A hundred times.

No, a million.

It's one thing I know I've never done and I want it so badly, but I also want it to be over. I want to look back on it. I want it safely in my memory where I can figure out what it means and how I did and whether I want to do it again.

Sayer is slowing down but I don't want him to slow down. But then I realize he's just letting me decide. He's letting me have control.

There's so little in my life I have control over.

And, yes. I want to control this.

I pull away from him.

He lifts his head up and he looks into my eyes, and in his green eyes for just a minute I see Lyle. For just a second I see Lyle.

Lyle. Why didn't I want you?

Why did you die?

Then he's said something else and I hear him this time. It's "I love you."

But for whatever reason—

This time, I don't believe him.

• • •

It's started raining.

Sayer uses the bathroom and when he comes back, I'm sitting up in the bed, my back propped against pillows.

I remember the wind making his windows rattle, but they don't rattle anymore. He must have fixed them.

He crawls into bed next to me and lies on his side.

"You should have gone home hours ago," he says. "It's late."

I shrug.

I'm not sure anymore what I should do versus what I shouldn't do. I'm not sure what's right and what's weird and what's comfortable and what's crazy.

The rain. The few candles scattered around the room, burning low in their jars. This feels right.

But I know what he means.

You turn a magnet over and it doesn't attract the same things. Suddenly it pushes away the things it connected with before, and if it's strong enough, it's impossible to get them to even touch.

There's something between them. It's invisible. But it has shape. It has a beginning and an end. You can't see it, but you feel it pushing back against your fingers.

"Are you doing okay?" I ask. I'm never the one to ask that and I realize I probably should, if I want the people I care about to keep caring about me.

"You mean Lyle?"

"I mean Lyle, yeah. Other things. Everything."

"I'm fine. It's weird. We were never close. But it's weird not having him around. And there are all these things I have to do. I have to cancel his cell phone. I have to sell his car and I have to cancel his insurance and I have to go to his bank and close his account. You never think about those things, you know. You never think about them."

"Where did he live?"

"With our uncle. He would have moved out when he turned eighteen. He wanted to live with me. Asked me a couple times. I didn't really have the room. He told me I could have moved. But we were never good under one roof."

Me in the picture couldn't have helped.

Was I something between them? Did I do irreparable damage to a relationship already fragile and unsteady? If I had kept both of them at arm's length, never made a choice between them. Or made the choice to take neither.

Am I awful?

Sometimes I feel like I'm awful.

Sayer, he guesses what I'm thinking. He puts a hand on my knee and he squeezes the bone.

"It was nothing you did."

"It was, sort of," I counter.

I can't deny my involvement, at least. I might not have been the nail but I was one last pound of the hammer.

"It wasn't anything you did," he says. He squeezes my knee again. Closes his eyes and sighs happily. Peacefully.

I have the feeling Sayer would stick up for me no matter

what I did. Drive a bus full of children into a lake and he'd be the one blaming the kids for being too loud.

I wonder how high my pedestal goes. It's undeserved, regardless. But the view. It's hard to give that up.

I settle down in the bed.

I don't want to sleep yet.

I want to go a little further backward. I want to remember more.

I'm with Sayer again.

We're standing in the doorway of his apartment. I have my car keys in my hand and my back is against the doorframe and he's going to kiss me for the first time.

This is when he kisses me for the first time.

I hold my breath for so long, I might have turned blue.

When he pulls away he puts his hand on the side of my face and pinches my skin between his fingers like he's checking if I'm real.

And he says my name.

He calls me Mabel.

He asks me not to go.

"Just stay a little longer, Mabel."

But it's a school night. My mother will kill me.

No no wait a minute.

I'm in Sayer's bed again. I stand up so quickly I almost lose my balance.

That's not my name.

Where have I heard that name before?

Mabel.

Lyle.

Lyle called me Mabel.

I pulled off his motorcycle helmet and he called me Mabel and I thought I heard him wrong.

I thought I heard him wrong but I didn't.

"Molly? What is it?"

Sayer must have fallen asleep because his eyes are red and bleary.

I take a step away from the bed and hit the bureau with my hips. Curse loudly and grab the wood with both my hands so I don't fall over. So I don't pass out. Because I don't know what this means but I think it must mean something big.

"What's going on?" he says again. He's sitting up now, rubbing his eyes with his fingers.

And carefully. As carefully as I can manage. With a voice even and steady and strong. I say, "Sayer. Who's Mabel?"

SIXTEEN.

"Tell me one thing about yourself," Sayer says. We're drinking coffee in a small, cluttered café. There's a stage against one wall big enough for a stool and a microphone. It's empty now; but in a few minutes Sayer's friend Parker will play a short set.

This is the first time Sayer took me here. I haven't met Parker yet.

Sayer buys me a cappuccino and he gets himself a coffee and we sit awkwardly, unsure. I play with my rings.

"One thing?" I say. "Just one thing?"

"For now," he says, smiling.

I don't know what to say so I take a long sip of my

cappuccino and when I pull the cup away Sayer looks at me, waiting.

"Like what?" I say. "Like what sort of thing?"

"Tell me your favorite color."

"My favorite color is red," I say.

"Huh," Sayer says. "Most girls say blue."

"So you ask a lot of girls?"

"I take polls on the street," he says, grinning. He has this grin. It's almost exactly like Lyle's. Only Lyle's is thinner. Lyle's is more sarcastic.

"Like a questionnaire? Do you have a questionnaire?" I ask.

"Yes. Um, favorite color. Favorite animal. How many brothers and sisters?" he says.

"Red. Cat. One brother and one sister."

"Names?"

"Clancy, Hazel."

"Are you close? Do you like them?"

"They're younger," I say. "We're close, I guess."

"How old are you?" Sayer asks.

"This is the fourth question," I say. "You said to tell you one thing. So it's my turn. What do you do?"

"I'm an electrician," Sayer says.

"Really?"

"Really. Well—I'm apprenticing."

"You're an apprentice?"

"Yeah."

"I don't think I've ever heard anyone call themselves an apprentice. It sounds like you practice magic."

Sayer smiles. He takes a quarter out of his pocket. He shows it to me. It's a regular quarter. He has me tap it on the table. He tells me to bite it, but I don't know where it's been. I give it back to him.

"Are you going to do a magic trick?" I ask, leaning back, waiting.

"Yeah, sure. I can do a magic trick. I just need a quarter. Got one?"

He's got his left hand in a fist. I reach for it and pry it open. The quarter's gone. I check the other hand. Gone.

"Impressive," I say.

"I'll do a trick. Let me borrow a quarter."

"I don't have a quarter."

"Sure you do. Look—I can see one. Hold out your hand."

I hold out my hand. He reaches behind my ear. He rubs his fingers together and the quarter falls into my palm.

"Do you do this to all the girls, too?" I ask.

"Yes," he says, frowning. "And they are generally more impressed by it than you are."

"Oh no, I'm impressed," I say, laughing. I try and give him back the quarter, but he pushes my hand away.

"Keep it," he says. "You can buy a gum ball."

I put the quarter on the table. Around me, people have started clapping. I look up at the stage; Parker is situating himself on the stool. He fixes the guitar strap around his neck and adjusts the microphone. The café goes quiet as he plays the first few notes of a song.

"I didn't think you were going to respond," Sayer says, suddenly close to me. I turn toward him; he's slid his chair next to mine so I can hear him over the music.

"I wasn't going to," I say. I turn back to the stage. Parker has dirty blond hair tucked behind his ears. He has a nice voice. He's singing about a girl.

"Because of my brother?" Sayer guesses.

I look at him again. His face is close to mine. I feel my heart lurch awkwardly, and for just a minute I feel myself slipping away. I grip my cappuccino mug and I stay here by sheer force of will.

"What makes you say that?" I ask.

"I saw you," Sayer says, "in the parking lot."

"Oh, yeah, when I fell."

"No. Well, yes, I saw that, too. I mean before that. I saw you before that."

"Right," I say. "Well."

"He likes you," he says.

"I gathered that."

"But you don't like him?"

"Not like—you know."

"Right. Why not?"

"I don't know. There's not really a reason."

"But you're friends."

"Of course."

"And so—"

"So I wasn't going to text you back," I say. "I wouldn't want him to find out. I don't know if that's . . . It feels kind of shitty. But I don't want him to know."

"He doesn't have to know."

"And you're okay with that? You're okay lying to him?"

"You have to talk to someone to lie to them," he says. It's almost sad, the way he says it. But then his face changes again and he's back to normal and he puts a finger on the rim of my mug. "Want another?"

"No, thanks."

"So what now?" he says.

"What do you mean, *what now*?"

"I mean—can I see you again?"

"Oh," I say. "Oh. Sure. When?"

"I don't know. Whenever."

"Oh. Sure. Sure, whenever. Yes."

"So?" Lyle says. We sit together at a picnic table. To our left, the big rock with the weathered green plaque I've never bothered to read. We're at Stage Fort Park. I like this park because there's ice cream nearby, and there's a good view of the ocean, dark blue and opening out in front of us like a painting.

There was a hurricane once, the last vestiges of a storm that hit the South hard and then crept up north, limping and spitting out the last of its winds. All the beaches around here were closed, but Molly and Luka and Erie snuck down to this park and stood under the big white gazebo and watched the shore get swallowed up by thick gray waves. Molly was terrified. She and Erie stood on either side of Luka and she flinched as the salt spray blew inland and got in her eyes and her hair and her mouth.

I loved it. The ocean looked like oil paint; it didn't look real. It looked like a made-up thing, all violent and shadowed and dangerous. I watched through Molly's eyes and I wanted to come out but I didn't. Back then, I never came out. Back then, I mostly watched.

"So, what?" I ask. A group of children climb the stairs behind the giant rock and emerge on top. I've always thought there should be some kind of railing, some kind of barrier to keep them all from plummeting over, but there isn't.

On the ground beside us, a father snaps a dozen photos in quick succession. Snap, snap, snap, snap. A mother waves frantically. Her hat blows off and she chases it down toward the beach.

"Sayer," Lyle says. "What do you think of Sayer, dummy?"

"Oh, Sayer," I say. "He was fine, right? He seems fine. He seems nice."

I achieve what I was aiming for—a blasé, whatever attitude. In actuality I have been thinking of Lyle's brother every day since I met him last week. I have been thinking about his small, neat apartment. I have been thinking about the hot water faucet in the bathroom that doesn't work. I have been thinking about the twig he pulled out of my hair. I have been thinking about the text message he sent me, the one I haven't yet responded to, the one the said:

> **Hey, Mabel. It's Sayer. It was nice to meet you.**

I don't know how Sayer got my phone number (got Molly's phone number, if we're being technical), but I read his message fourteen times in Spanish class and then I deleted it before I let Molly come back out. And then the rest of that day I just repeated it in my head and I thought about his eyes, which are green, almost the same shade as Lyle's eyes but different—lighter, maybe. Wider. Nicer.

"Huh," Lyle says, and I realize he's been staring at me.

"Huh," I repeat, nudging his shoulder with my shoulder. "What's that supposed to mean?"

"Nothing," he says, shrugging.

"How come you aren't that close?" I ask.

"Who says we're not close?"

"You said it. You said it multiple times, actually. You said, 'Mabel, we're going to meet my brother. We're not that close, but—'"

"Okay, okay," he says, laughing. "I get it." He thinks for a minute. "I don't know. I've never really thought about it."

"What about when you were younger?"

"Before my parents died, maybe," he says.

He's never told me how his parents died, but I know he was nine when it happened.

"What then?" I say. "I mean—after they died. Why did you stop being close?"

"We grew up in different homes," Lyle said. "I went to live with my uncle, my mother's brother. Sayer went with our father's parents."

"How come you were split up?"

"Neither of them could afford us. Both of us," Lyle says. "So we didn't see that much of each other."

"What about now that Sayer has his own place?"

Lyle scowls and shrugs and rests his elbows on the picnic table. He squints out over the water.

"I wanted to move in with him. He said he couldn't afford it. I said—I wanted to drop out of high school and go to work, too. But he said no."

"You can't drop out of high school," I say.

"Says who?"

"Says me."

"What do you know? Your parents are still alive," Lyle says.

I don't know what that has to do with anything, but you can't argue with dead parents. Lyle doesn't say anything for a long time and then he stands up and looks back at me, suspicious.

"So you think he's nice?" he says.

"No," I say. "I take it back. He seems like a jerk."

Lyle smiles, even though he has to know I'm joking.

"Yeah," he agrees, "he is."

Lyle wants to introduce me to his brother, and for some reason I'm nervous.

I know he has a brother of course, he's mentioned him before, but that doesn't mean I want to meet him. He'll just be one more person I have to be careful around. Sometimes, with Lyle, it's so hard to stay focused. To stay in the moment, to not fade out. But I can't let that happen. I can't mess this up. Lyle's the only friend I have, the only friend I've made by myself and kept by myself and I can't lose him.

So I'll have to meet his brother because that's what he wants me to do.

It's April and the weather's still cold, still wet and gray and miserable.

Lyle drives me to Sayer's apartment and I ask the same questions over and over again.

"Have you told him anything about me?"

"I try not to mention you."

"No, really? What have you said?"

"I said you're my friend. I haven't told him anything else."

"Did you say how we met?"

"I said we met at my job. I served you a cup of coffee

and you complained it was too cold. Threw an impressive tantrum and stormed out. Came back the next day to apologize and it was like you were a completely different person."

A completely different person.

Lyle, the comedian.

I scowl at him and he laughs. He thinks he's the funniest person in the universe.

"Will you relax?" he says. "He doesn't know anything. He's just my brother, Mabel, and I'd really like you to meet him."

This satisfies me temporarily and I relax a little, pulling my jacket, which I have spread over me like a blanket, closer to my chin. Lyle's heater barely works, and today his car feels as warm as an icebox. He wanted to take the motorcycle. In hindsight, it might have been warmer.

"Do you think he'll like me?" I ask.

I mean it as a joke, sort of, but I'm also a little serious. I've never had to worry about it before. What if I like him and he doesn't like me? Will he like me just because Lyle likes me? Is that how brothers work? Will I be accepted by default? I only have Clancy to base my guesses on, and he's not a good example. He basically hates everyone, friends of mine or not.

"He'll like you, trust me," Lyle says.

"How do you know?"

"Because you're pretty, I guess."

"He'll like me because I'm pretty?"

"And you're sort of smart."

"You guess I'm pretty and I'm sort of smart?"

"If you try not to speak so much, he'll probably like you," Lyle finishes, laughing to himself.

"What's he like?" I say.

"He looks like me," Lyle says, shrugging. "People always say that. He's older, you know. Not as funny. Not as clever. Not as . . . What's this word I'm searching for?"

"Moronic?"

"*Dashing*, Mabel. He's not as dashing."

I try and picture an older, less funny, less dashing Lyle, but I come up blank.

"Have you told him about me?"

"Are we doing this again?" Lyle asks, shooting me a look as he puts his blinker on and turns into the driveway of a large Victorian house.

"This is where he lives?" I say, impressed.

"Not in the whole house," Lyle says quickly. "It's all apartments now. And it's small. His apartment is small."

I feel butterflies in the pit of my stomach that I attribute to the basic nerves of meeting someone new.

But there's something else.

He does look like Lyle. Only taller and kinder. His face less thin and his eyes more green.

I found a picture in Lyle's wallet. I don't know why I never told him, but I have the feeling he would have been angry. There's a lot of resentment between them, although that's not saying much. Sometimes I think Lyle resents the whole world.

But the picture was nice. Sayer looked nice. Not anything like the boys in my high school. Not anything like any boy I've met before.

"Why do you look so weird?" Lyle asks.

"I'm weird," I say. "Weird people look weird."

He parks the car, kills the engine. He looks like he wants to say something, but I get out of the car before he gets the chance.

He's parked at the back end of the small lot. It's bordered by a patch of trees and I'm ankle-deep in brush. Great spot, Lyle.

I pick my way out of the mess as carefully as I can and come around the back of the car, where he's waiting for me with a funny expression on his face.

"Hey," he says.

"What, Lyle?"

"Can't I just say hey?"

"Can't you just find a better spot to park next time?"

He takes a step closer to me.

I sort of always knew we'd come to this, despite my dropping as many hints as possible that I will never share his romantic feelings about us.

"Lyle, hey, wait a second."

"Just . . . just hold on, Mabel. You can't tell me there's nothing—"

"There's nothing! Okay? I'm sorry. Lyle, there's nothing."

He stops for a minute and then his face sets into a strong line of resolve and he takes another step toward me and pushes his face against my face, kissing me with such enthusiasm I forget, for a few seconds, that I'm supposed to be pulling away.

Then I recover and I step back quickly, directly into the brush that immediately catches around my ankle. I'm propelled backward into an impressive batch of brambles that claw eagerly at my skin.

I land hard on my ass.

Lyle, to his credit, doesn't look particularly sad that I've shirked his advances. Rather, he bursts out laughing, making no move to help me up and holding his stomach while tears slide down his face.

I haven't put my jacket on so my arms are bare and covered in scratches. Beads of blood pop up and I wet a finger with my tongue, dab them away one by one.

Finally Lyle realizes I'm still on the ground and he pulls me up in one jerky motion. Together, we pull briars out of my shirt and he uses his sleeve to dab away the blood and dirt I've missed.

"Lyle?" says a new voice, and my stomach drops a mile as I see him striding across the parking lot. He looks like his picture. He looks as nice as his picture. "Lyle, what the hell are you doing? Trying to hide her body? You know you have to kill her first?"

Oh, ha-ha.

"Knew I'd mixed up the order somewhere," Lyle says, shaking his head.

Sayer pushes past him and sticks his hand out for me to shake, which I do. He smiles and I feel my stomach lift slightly. He has a nice smile.

"Hey," he says. "You must be Mabel."

"It's nice to meet you," I say.

He pulls his hand away and brings it up to my head. I don't know what he's doing but then he's pulled something out of my hair and is holding it out in front of me.

It's a twig.

So basically, I've made a great first impression.

Lyle laughs like an idiot and starts off toward the house.

It's just Sayer and me alone for a minute in this parking lot, him holding a twig he just pulled out of my hair and me with my arms burning where all the brambles attacked me.

He doesn't say anything. He smiles. He tosses the twig away and then he puts his arm around my shoulders and we follow Lyle inside.

SEVENTEEN.

Okay. Just breathe.

Just breathe, just breathe, just breathe.

The world is tilting violently and white spots are dancing in my vision. Sayer has pulled himself up and now sits perched on the edge of the bed. I'm holding my hand out to him, palm away.

Don't come any closer.

In my head is a thrumming, getting louder and louder with each second. It's like the feedback on a speaker or the echo of thunder.

I close my eyes but when my eyes are closed the spinning is worse so I open them wide. Sayer is looking at me, concern etched in every line of his face.

Lyle called me Mabel.

I called Alex on the phone and he said my name like a question. Like he was checking to see who I was.

Mabel.

Lyle called me Mabel. Sayer called me Mabel.

"Wait," I say. Sayer's off the bed. He takes a step toward me. "Just wait."

The pieces are beginning to fall into place.

The blackouts. The missing time. The secret. The thing that everybody seems to know.

Hazel, watching me on the couch.

Of course she would be the first to notice.

She notices everything.

"Molly?"

"Wait."

The twigs in my hair.

The scratches on my arms.

I had been so scared. Did someone hurt me? Was I in danger?

But, no. I had fallen into a patch of brambles. Cut my skin on sticks and stones.

Woken up that night in the middle of a history essay. Almost done with my homework and I remembered nothing of the past four hours.

It was almost as if someone else had taken a turn at living my life.

Someone else.

And suddenly the answer hangs waiting in the air in front of me.

I could reach up and pluck it from the atmosphere.

Someone else living my life.

I don't feel anyone else inside me.

But what else accounts for it?

What else accounts for any of it?

"Molly?"

"Wait," I repeat, but quieter this time. This time barely a whisper escapes my throat.

I'm remembering something else. Something that happened to me. I had never given it a second thought.

I walked into Alex's office one day and went to sit down in my usual chair but found a book in my way. I picked it up. The cover was a woman's face cut into a dozen vertical pieces. *Sybil*.

"What's this?" I asked, tossing it on his desk.

He looked up like he'd forgotten it was there. Reached for it, shook his head, and chuckled.

"My last patient borrowed it. Must have forgotten to tell me he was done. It's a good book, you know. You might like it."

"Never heard of it."

"It's about a woman living with sixteen separate personalities. All trapped inside her head. Fascinating case."

"It was a movie or something, right?" I asked, feigning

interest to make Alex happy. All those psychology books bored me to death. He'd tried to get me to read some in the past and they only succeeded in putting me to sleep.

"It's been the basis for a couple movies. You should read it, Molly. You might find it interesting."

I had woken up two hours later.

Why had I woken up two hours later?

Had Mabel come out to see what Alex knew about split personalities? Had he known, then, about her? He must have. That look on his face was too forced. Too offhanded. Too clever. He'd left the book there on purpose.

"Molly?" Sayer says again and this time I lower my hand and look at him.

"Who's Mabel?" I say again. Even though I know. I know who Mabel is now and maybe I've known all along.

"I'm not supposed to—"

"I have to go. It's fine, I have to go."

I find my sweater, pull it on and go into the kitchen. The clock on the microwave says two a.m.

I can't go home now. But I have to. I have to see something.

Sayer follows me. He tries to take my hand but I pull away from him, find my shoes and put them on, hopping, one by one.

I don't know who you are.

And I'm certainly not the girl you know.

"Molly, please don't leave this late. Please just stay until morning. We can talk, okay? Please don't leave."

I don't want to talk. I just want to get out of this apartment, get into my car, and drive home.

There is something I have to do. Something I have to see.

"It's fine, Sayer. I'm fine. Okay? I'll call you tomorrow."

"Text me when you get home at least, okay? Let me know you're safe?"

"Sure. Sure, I will."

Outside, the night is unforgiving. Cold and windy with quick bursts of rain. I get soaked on the way to my car, but then it stops and I drive with the windows open to keep myself awake. I'm shaking and my teeth are chattering drumbeats in my mouth when I finally get to my driveway.

My parents haven't left any lights on.

I use my cell phone like a flashlight but still trip up the front steps and only just manage to catch myself on the railing.

I've shut my brain off. I'm moving through the house with no obvious brain functions other than those that are absolutely necessary. Take a step. Take another step. Open this door. Step through the door. Cross the room and open the cabinet underneath the TV.

This is where my parents keep the photo albums. I've turned on every light in the living room without really realizing it. I spread the albums across the floor in chronological order. One summer, in the middle of one of her frequent bouts of organizational inspiration, my mother sorted every single photograph in the house. She put them all into identical green albums. She wrote the corresponding years on the front in thick black magic marker. Hazel and I were supposed to help, but we mostly just looked through picture after picture, finding every naked photo of baby Clancy that we could and making one big collage on the carpet, ecstatic at our cleverness.

But there was one thing I kept noticing.

In the photographs of me.

It wasn't every photo. It wasn't even most of them. But every so often I'd find one, pull it out of the big shoe box where all the pictures sat messy and unorganized before my mom got to them. And I would look at this picture of myself. Me with my arm around Hazel. Me in midjump on my bed. Me hanging an ornament on the Christmas tree.

And it was like.

I don't know.

It was like I was looking at someone else. It was like I was looking at someone who looked exactly like me. She had my hair and she was my height and she had the birthmark on my arm. She was me. Except she wasn't.

And I couldn't explain it. So I put them all away. And even though I told myself it was nothing, wasn't there a small voice in the back of my head? Wasn't there something nudging at the corners of my brain, something telling me to look deeper, investigate further? Wasn't there something telling me they weren't nothing. That they didn't mean nothing. That they meant everything.

I want to find those photos now, to see if they contain any evidence, any clue. To see if they make sense. Do they confirm anything? Or is it just my overactive imagination finding things where they don't actually exist? Creating panic where panic isn't needed.

I flip through album after album. I pull open the covers and scour over every year from my birth to the present.

But I can't find any of those photos.

Where did they all go?

Did I just imagine them?

I start over. I get to my sixth birthday party, the year Clancy put his entire face in the cake, when I hear a movement behind me. I jump a mile and turn around.

It's my mom.

"I wasn't at Erie's," I say. I guess I'm crying because my voice is all thick and wrong.

"I know," she says, "you were with Sayer."

"How did you—"

"He texted me when you left. I've been waiting up for you, Molly. I was worried."

"I'm sorry I lied to you," I say.

She nods. "What are you looking for?"

But she sounds like she knows what I'm looking for. And that's when I notice the shoe box in her hands.

"You knew about her?" I say. I wipe my face with my

sleeve and maybe I try to stand up but I feel rooted to this spot on the carpet, the mess of albums spread out in front of me like a halo.

"Not at first," she says. She takes a couple steps into the room but she seems unsure where to go. She surveys the carpet and sighs. "There were hints, when you were younger. You'd ask me questions you should have known the answers to. Once you woke up one morning and asked who decorated the Christmas tree. When it was you, of course. I mean, we all did. But you were there."

"Why didn't you tell someone?"

"I never thought . . . It was always little things, you know. And even then, Molly, you were so good at pretending to be okay. And besides, it went away."

"It did?"

"When you were about ten or eleven. You stopped asking weird questions. And whenever I looked at you, I knew it was really you. Before . . . well, sometimes I wasn't sure."

"And then?"

She takes a few more steps and sits on her knees in front of me. "And then things got a little rough. About a year ago. We made the decision to—well, we strongly suggested you start seeing someone."

Strongly suggested is a funny choice of words because what actually happened was my parents loaded me into the minivan and drove me to Alex's office. There wasn't a suggestion involved. They didn't tell me where we were going until we were in the parking lot. I thought we were headed to the bookstore; they told me a big shipment had just come in. I'd spent five minutes arguing in the foyer about how much homework I had to do, and why couldn't they take Hazel or Clancy instead of me? But, no, they said, it had to be me, and before I knew it I was being shepherded into Alex's office and I was shaking his hand and my parents were saying, *Now, we'll just be in the waiting room, Molly. We'll just be out here, okay?*

My mother sighs.

"In retrospect, we should have taken you there so much earlier. We should have been paying more attention; we should have noticed something."

I told Clancy everyone would be better off without me and my parents had taken me to see a shrink and he had told me to call him Alex. *Just call me Alex,* he'd said. *I'll call you Molly.*

"It didn't take him very long to . . . to meet her," my mother continues. She looks impossibly sad; she looks impossibly guilty. "And when he told us . . . well, that particular explanation had never crossed our minds."

"These are the pictures?" I say, reaching for the shoe box. She relinquishes it at once.

"Of Mabel," she says. "They used to be in the albums, of course. But a couple months ago, she asked me to take them out. I told her . . ." Her voice chokes. She puts a hand over her mouth. "I told her these were our family albums, and she was family. But she wanted to take them out. So we sat down together and we went through every one and she pulled out all the photos of her. Some of them, I couldn't even tell. But she knew them all."

"Why? Did she say why?"

"She said she wanted them to be in one place. So you could see them all, when you were ready. And then you could decide what you wanted to do."

"She said I'd ask for them?"

"She knew you very well. I think she was getting ready to say good-bye," my mom says. There's a sadness in her voice but it's a sadness that's unsure of its place. She doesn't know where to put it; she doesn't know where it came from or how it works.

"Open it," she says. "See what you think."

What I think. I don't know what I think. I don't know about anything, but I open the shoe box and I pull out the first photograph.

Me, riding a bike in the driveway. Shooting a big, sloppy grin to the camera.

No. Not me. Pixit.

Mabel. Kenzie.

I can see that now.

I was lucide Dec 15 2018

EIGHTEEN.

"Are you serious with this shit, Alex?" I say, grabbing the book from his hands and holding it up as evidence.

My transition is fluid. If you are not paying very close attention, you miss it.

It takes Alex a moment to figure it out.

"Molly?" he asks tentatively.

He'll never say my name first because if it isn't me, Molly will be wondering why he's calling her Mabel.

That was my idea.

"She's not ready to find out," I say, tossing the book back on his desk. "And she won't find out like this. *Sybil,*

Alex, really? Could you be more obvious?"

"Maybe if she read it—"

"I won't let her find out like that." I sit down in the chair, cross my arms over my chest. He makes me so mad sometimes I could scream. He doesn't know what's best for her. Only I know what's best for her. "Besides," I add, "they're saying the shrink made the whole thing up."

"Largely fabricated," Alex corrects me. "Exaggerated. And you know I don't like the term *shrink*."

"Whatever. I just thought we had agreed that we don't tell her until I say she's ready."

"Mabel."

I'm about to get one of his lectures. I can tell by the way he says my name. I get up from the chair, having no desire to be trapped in it while he reprimands me. I go to the window. It's spring. The air is almost warm enough.

"I know her better than you," I say. My preemptive strike.

"I have no doubt about that, Mabel," he says.

"Can you stop saying my name like it will validate me or something? I know my own name; I've had it my whole life," I snap.

"You're upset."

"Of course I'm upset. We had a deal and now you're trying to tell her behind my back!"

"I'm not telling her," he says.

"What is that, then? What's that book?" I say, pointing at it.

"I'm giving her the tools to figure it out for herself."

"I told you I'll tell her, Alex! But you have to give me time, okay? You have to trust me. She's not ready yet."

Alex sits on the edge of his desk and watches me. He's always been a little wary of me. But I guess that's fair.

To him, everything is my fault.

Molly's illness.

They don't call it a split personality or multiple personality disorder anymore. It's dissociative identity disorder. And he thinks it's all my fault.

Well, it's not, Alex.

You've read that book; you should know.

It's Molly's fault. She made me.

She wasn't whole enough on her own. She made me to fill herself out. She made me to stick into the corners of her body, to take up room, to be complete.

"When do you think she'll be ready?" he says.

"I don't know."

"Next month? Next fall? Next year?"

"I don't know! I said I don't know."

"You're hiding an awful lot from her. It's always been my opinion that honesty is the most important aspect to successful therapy."

"Honesty, sure." I snort. "Look, Alex, you don't know what she's like. She doesn't want to know, okay? She *refuses* to know. It's not always me! Sometimes she makes me come out. Sometimes she pushes herself away. She worms down into the very bottom of our body and she stays there until I've made everything safe again."

The word *safe*.

I know that's what Alex is dwelling on because he looks away from me. He looks down at his own hands and he won't meet my eyes until at least two full minutes have passed.

"Safe?" he repeats. He tries hard to keep the judgment out of his voice but, hey, even shrinks are human.

"All I've ever done is to keep Molly safe," I say through my teeth.

"That's not how I see things," he says.

I go and sit in the chair.

Might as well.

All my anger has dissipated.

In his eyes I'm the reason we're here in the first place. I might as well behave. Get the most out of it. I could try and hand things back to Molly, but she's definitely not willing. The book thing upset her. She has no idea why, but some things just get under our skin.

"I don't expect you to understand," I say.

"Can you explain to me, then—"

"I have my reasons for everything. I don't have to tell you."

"So don't tell me. But you do know I can get her the medication? I can give it to her parents; they can slip it to her so she doesn't even know she's taking it. So you don't even know. I can make you go away, Mabel. If you don't cooperate."

"If you don't trust me, do it," I say. "Do it. And see how long she lasts without me."

I stand up. Our time is up and I feel sick.

I'm halfway to the door before he says, "I do trust you, Mabel. I trust you implicitly. I trust you with Molly's life."

"Good. Because her life is my life, and you have to help her. But you can't do it without me. If you give up on me, you give up on her."

Just a moment of calm between us. The air in the room relaxes; I breathe for the first time in minutes. A hint of a smile on Alex's mouth.

"Day or night," he says.

"I know."

And I leave.

Somehow the next two days pass and it's Saturday. My mother lets me sleep late. She must have spoken to Clancy and Hazel; they're avoiding me like I'm infectious. My father tiptoes past my doorway like he's terrified I'll pop out screaming.

I thought I had control over the memories, but Mabel isn't gone.

She isn't gone yet. And she's the one pressing play.

Other than that, she keeps her distance. She doesn't come out anymore. She doesn't answer the questions I shout inside my head. They reverberate against the walls of my skull and fall untouched to the tips of my toes.

The time I woke up a few miles from New York?

Alex had threatened to put me on drugs.

"Just watch what I'll do," she had said. "Just watch what I'll do to her."

But you can't really call it kidnapping, can you?

You can't kidnap your own body.

I do research online. Mabel is called my alter. She is omniscient. Some alters are and some aren't. The blackouts are normal. I can't remember what she does. And it's also normal that I can't feel her.

I can't feel her.

I wake up Saturday to the memory of Mabel and Alex's fight over the book. I can't deny the fire in her voice, the flame in her eyes.

She's so different from me.

She gets angrier than I do and she's louder than I am and her voice even sounds different. Not like an accent, exactly, but a lilt. A limp.

Me, I always sound like I've given up on my sentences halfway through them. And how can I expect anyone else to believe me if I can't believe myself?

The memories change. They move into early spring and stretch back to late winter. Lyle and I are inseparable. We go everywhere together; I cling to him like a lifeline.

Mabel clings to him like a lifeline.

He's self-centered and full of himself and loud and obnoxious but he loves her. He loves her and she chose someone else.

His brother, of all people.

Snow falls and every memory I have brings me closer and closer to whatever happened a year ago, to whatever brought Lyle and Mabel together.

I know she'll tell me. She'll let me see it bit by bit until I'm ready to understand.

Which means waiting. It means reliving every detail until I get to the day in question.

So I pay attention to my relationship with Lyle. I watch as we progress backward from best friends who sort of hate each other to best friends who love each other to best friends who are unsure of how close they are. How close they're supposed to be and how close they're getting.

Mabel teaches Lyle, laughing, how to braid her hair and he shows her how to play his favorite video game and they spend hours drinking soda, shooting bad guys.

When Sayer texts me, I don't answer.

It's not me you love.

And if Mabel doesn't want to talk to you, I have no business talking to you either.

When Erie calls me late on Saturday morning, I tell her to come over. I take a quick shower and I knock on Hazel's door, wrapped in a towel with my hair dripping onto the carpet.

She's reading a book on her bed, her head propped up on pillows and one leg crossed over the other. She jumps up when she sees me.

"Molly. Hi," she says.

"Hey."

"Do you need something?"

"Are you busy?"

"No," she says. She lays the book down on the comforter. "No, what's up?"

"Do my hair?" I ask. "And, um—pick out something I can wear?"

She sits at my window while I change. A blue patterned dress with a darker blue cardigan. I leave it unbuttoned and then I sit on the floor in front of her and she braids my hair.

Once Hazel told me that if I kept secrets from her, she'd keep secrets from me.

Once Hazel told me that, yes, I acted different sometimes. But nobody could tell except her.

When she finishes braiding my hair, she sits back on the window seat.

"Mabel said bye," she says.

Of course Mabel would say good-bye to my sister.

You can't leave my sister without saying good-bye. She demands to be acknowledged.

"When?" I ask. I turn around to look at her.

"The other night. After you'd gone to bed. I think she does that a lot, so you won't be able to tell."

"That's sneaky."

"She has to be sneaky," Hazel says.

Erie gets here a few minutes later. She lets herself in and we sit on my bed, exchanging stories. Mostly, she tells me about Mabel. How she never noticed. When she found out, she was shocked.

I'm not surprised. I doubt Erie notices a quarter of the things she's supposed to. And like Hazel said, Mabel's sneaky.

She asks me about Sayer.

I tell her, I don't know. I think we're done.

There's not much to say after that.

She leaves that night, after lunch and dinner, and I clear up the plates in the kitchen as my parents and Hazel settle down in the living room to watch a movie.

Upstairs, I change into pajamas and spend a while cleaning up my room. Putting clothes away, bringing dirty water glasses down to the kitchen. Finally it's good enough and I'm just about to get into bed when someone knocks on my door and Clancy pushes into the room before I have a chance to answer.

I sit cross-legged as he walks around touching things, avoiding what he so obviously wants to say.

"Listen, Molly," he begins, but then he stops. He sits down on the bed with me and he looks like he wants to take my hand but he doesn't. "How far have you gotten?"

He doesn't say much.

But when he does . . .

I'm crying before I even realize it.

"He was my friend," I whisper. "Clancy, he was my friend."

How far have I gotten?

Far enough to properly feel the loss of the boy on the motorcycle.

Far enough to miss him.

Far enough to grieve.

NINETEEN.

"**Y**ou shouldn't drink so much, Lyle," I say. He's got a bottle of whiskey tucked into an inside pocket of his coat. I know it's there even though he's been trying to hide it from me. He doesn't like when I tell him what to do, but you know what, Lyle? Tough shit. Friends have to tell each other what to do sometimes, and you're so insistent on being my friend. Well, this is the cost.

"Relax, Mabel. It's the weekend," he says.

It's Thursday.

I'm about to point that out to him when he takes a false step and I watch as his foot goes out from under him. He lands waist deep in a pile of snow and I'm dying laughing as he tries to worm his way out of the drift.

What he's trying to do is climb up a snowbank to reach a broken window in this warehouse. The snow's so deep it's covered up the door, and all the ground-floor windows are boarded shut.

It was my idea to come back here, so I can't say anything.

"Little help!" he demands, and I start digging him out with my hands. I'm not wearing gloves, so it's only a matter of minutes before my fingers are completely numb. By the time I get him out, he's so cold he can't bend his legs and fresh snow has started to fall from the gray November sky.

Coldest one on record since sometime in the seventies.

"Oh come on, Lyle, forget it," I say. My face is red and my fingers are aching and inside my boots, I can't feel my toes anymore.

"You want to get inside, we're getting inside," Lyle says. He has his mouth set in a line of grim determination, which might be impressive were his teeth not currently chattering.

"It's really fine. I'm fine. We can go watch a movie or something. Find someplace warm."

"Around back," he says, "I think there's another way in. We drove all the way out here, we might as well try."

I attempt a shrug but find my shoulders unresponsive, frozen stiff inside my insufficient jacket.

Lyle has already started off around the far end of the building, so I jog to keep up with him, hoping the sudden movement will start the blood flowing in my veins. Apparently he has the same idea as me, because suddenly we're running full speed around the warehouse, laughing and pelting each other with snowballs and tripping and falling and getting up again. I think I almost break my ankle, but it's so cold I can't even feel it.

The warehouse is big. It takes us a few minutes to reach the other side, and by now the snow is falling in earnest and there's a clean sheet of white over everything. It occurs to me that my car will be covered by the time we get back to it but I don't care about that. The roads, too, they'll be a mess, but all I want is to get inside this warehouse.

When I first mentioned it, I expected Lyle to throw a fit. Why would I want to come back here, right?

I don't know.

That's the truth.

I've never been an overly sentimental person, which I guess comes from being Molly's hidden half. I've never had anything to be sentimental about. Everything I own is Molly's. My favorite pair of shoes? They're Molly's. My favorite book? It's on Molly's bookshelf. My favorite place to sit? By the window in Molly's bedroom.

Hard to be sentimental when you have nothing to be sentimental about.

I tried to keep a journal once, but I wasn't good at that either.

What would I write in it?

Had a few hours today to watch TV.

Helped decorate the Christmas tree. They thought I was Molly.

Had five minutes to send a text to Lyle. Gotta erase it quick before Molly comes back and sees it.

I should have been a spy in another life.

There's no one better than me at avoiding detection.

But it's fine. So I'm not sentimental. But why the warehouse? Why bother coming back here?

I don't know.

Only there's no place else in the entire world that I have. That I have, and that Molly knows nothing about.

The warehouse is mine.

And what a prize it is.

Drafty and big and dangerous and half falling apart in places.

But it's mine.

And alters can't be choosy.

Ahead of me, Lyle slips again but catches himself before he goes down. We've come around the other side of the building now and I see the door before he does. I've stopped running but I start again, pushing past him with a laugh and sprinting for it. Even from here I can see it's all rotted. Even from here I can see how fragile it is. How a few good kicks will bring it down.

He's by my side in a flash and we work at it together, kicking our frozen feet against the old, termite-eaten wood. Each impact sends a bolt of pain up my leg, and I wonder briefly about frostbite, about freezing to death.

With an impressive rip, the bottom half of the door collapses inward.

Just enough room to wiggle underneath.

I go first with Lyle right behind me, pushing my butt as I swat at his hands like they're flies.

It's fairly light inside. The upper windows aren't boarded and most of them are cracked in places, so it's freezing but the snow acts like a hundred tiny mirrors and sends blinding rays of light inside.

"Over here," Lyle says.

This was his place before it was mine. He knows it better than I do and I follow close behind him as he leads me deep into its labyrinthine belly. We pass people, dark shapes huddled under blankets, faces peering out at us, eyes lost in shadow and just the tip of a nose visible. Lyle puts his arm around my shoulders and nobody bothers us. They know him. He is the boy who brings them bread and cheese sandwiches. He is the boy who brings them bottles of water, who pleads with them to go to the shelter in town. Get a shower; spend the night in a bed. But the snow is their shower, they say. These blankets, this floor. This is their bed.

One man calls Lyle by name and we stop for a minute outside his house. You have to call it a house. There is an old metal office desk, a chair. A tarp for a roof. A bed and a pile of magazines. Everything is neat and organized. When I came here for the first time, I was by myself. This man is the only one who introduced himself. He asked me if I needed anything.

What I needed, I couldn't take from him.

The man holds out a cup and Lyle tips a generous amount of whiskey into it.

The man's name is Sport. That's what he calls himself.

Lyle says, "All right, Sport?"

And Sport says, "All right, Lyle."

We go deeper into the pit of the warehouse.

The homeless people dwindle in numbers and the junkies appear, their gaunt faces shining out of the shadows like flashlights. They slink away from us. They know Lyle, too, but they can't be bothered with him and he can't be bothered with them.

They're harmless, he told me once. They're harmless if you don't look them in the eyes or stay too long in their corridors.

Upstairs now and it gets brighter. My breath comes out in puffs of smoke but there's a fire up ahead.

This fire, it never goes out.

There's a girl standing in front of it now, throwing small pieces of wood into the trash can to keep the blaze alive. She's small and thin, about our age, with a cheerful, skinny face.

The runaways.

I don't know this girl but she bolts toward Lyle with a face lit up and beaming and she throws her arms around his neck.

"Thought you were dead!" she squeals, and I'm reminded of Hazel. This girl is an older, more desperate Hazel. I feel protective of her immediately. When she pulls away from Lyle and looks at me, I stick my hand out.

"Mabel," I say.

Lyle told me I had to always introduce myself first with the runaways. Otherwise they wouldn't trust me.

"Susan," she says. "Where'd you go, Lyle, huh? Haven't seen you since the raid."

Every couple weeks there's a raid. Everybody clears out for a few hours, then scurries back in like mice.

The last raid was the last time I was here. Two months ago, which is a good long quiet streak for them.

"Been busy," Lyle says, shrugging.

He's different here. I notice it right away. He talks differently and he holds his body differently.

"Couple people got locked up for a few days," Susan says. "Dinky and Pretty and Alice. Thought you might be in, too."

"Too fast," Lyle says, and smiles.

No, that's not true, Lyle. You didn't get caught because you were with me.

"I think it was good for Pretty, anyway," she continues, smiling. "You know how he gets."

"I know," Lyle says. "He here?"

"It's almost Thanksgiving," she says, and the smile fades from her face. "Nobody's here except me."

"And us, now. Look, I brought you something," Lyle says. He starts pulling stuff from his jacket I didn't even know he had. A box of crackers, a wedge of cheese. The bottle of whiskey and a ziplock baggie of chocolate chip cookies. He spreads them on the floor like a banquet, steps back, and holds out his hands. "Eh?"

"I can always count on you," she says. She's smiling again and she's so much like Hazel that I want to reach out and hug her, bring her home, and give her something better to eat and somewhere warm to sleep. "They'll be back in a couple days, anyway. Nice to have the place to myself."

We eat together on the floor. We take small bites and let Susan have most of it. We split the whiskey three ways and we laugh and tell stupid jokes and the warehouse gets darker but the fire is bright and hot and I even take my coat off.

Lyle told me he came here for a while after his parents died. He was only nine. He stayed two weeks with the runaways until Sayer found him and dragged him out.

But he's never really left.

He comes back with food and booze, and I know that besides Sayer, this is his real family. There's a revolving door of runaways here, but all runaways are the same. That's what he told me.

After the last of the cheese is done, Susan curls up next to the fire in a dozen mismatched blankets and falls instantly asleep. Lyle and I sit cross-legged on the floor exchanging the last few sips of whiskey.

I didn't bring him here to tell him, but it's as good a time as any. I take the empty bottle in my hand and spin it around on the floor so I'll have something to do. When it stops spinning it's pointing at him, and he pretends like he's going to kiss me and I laugh and push him away. But then I guess my face changes and he stops moving and waits for me to say something.

"Look," I start. My hands are shaking and I sit on them.

I've never told anyone before. Besides Alex, sure. He doesn't count.

I don't know how to say it.

I'm not a real person, Lyle.

Or, I'm not exactly a real person.

I'm a shadow.

I'm a copy.

I'm a fake.

When I was little, I used to fantasize about having my own body. Molly and I are the same age and when we were four and five and six I was fine with it. But then we turned seven. Something about seven, I don't know.

Suddenly I wanted more.

I wanted to be by myself. I wanted to be like Molly, who didn't have to hear my voice in her head all the time.

I always heard her. I saw her dreams and I heard her seven-year-old thoughts and I felt her pain and I felt her jubilation. But it wasn't mine. It wasn't my happiness and it wasn't my sadness and I wanted my own.

I would rather have never been born. But now that I'm here, I want more.

But Molly never thought about that.

She's the one who made me.

She's the one who split herself in half and pushed me away from her. Pushed me down real deep inside her until she couldn't even feel me anymore.

Sometimes I think she's a real fucking bitch, but without her I have nothing.

Without her, I can't even walk across a room.

"Mabel?" Lyle says.

I guess I'm crying. I hardly ever cry. They're borrowed tears. Even these don't belong to me. I wipe my cheeks and then I laugh. A sharp, piercing laugh that echoes around the warehouse like a bird.

"I have something to tell you," I say. "And it's really fucking weird."

"How weird?" he says.

"That first time I met you?" I say. "That was the first time I met anyone."

TWENTY.

The day I met Lyle. That day. Molly goes to school.

She goes to school. She fails a test. She forgets an English essay sitting on her bed. She gets into a fight with Luka about something stupid, about a party he wants her to go to. She spills spaghetti sauce on her shirt.

It is a white shirt. It is new. She tries to wash it in the bathroom, but it only makes the stain bigger and more watery. She spends six minutes crying on the toilet. She is late to health class. They are learning CPR.

That day she drives with Clancy to the middle school. They wait for Hazel in the parking lot. She drives her brother and sister home and she goes into her room and she cries again and she thinks to herself—I hear her, I hear everything—she thinks to herself *I can't live on this earth anymore. I can't live on this planet. I just can't fucking do it. I just can't, I just can't, I just can't.*

Clancy comes into her room. He wants her to drive him to his friend's house.

"Are you crying?" he asks. He stands in the doorway and watches her on her bed. She wipes her cheeks and stands up and turns away from him and straightens her comforter.

"Get out, Clancy."

"Are you okay?" he says.

"Clancy—get out. Please get out."

"I just need a ride," he says. "Can you drive me to Tom's?"

"Please, please, please," she says. "Please, get out. Please, please get out."

She covers her face with her hands. He stands in the doorway. She turns around. She doesn't look sad anymore. She looks angry.

"Molly, it's five streets over. It'll take you three minutes."

"Walk," she says. "You can walk. I'm busy."

"What are you doing? What are you busy doing?"

"I'm busy."

"It's cold outside. I'm not going to walk. It'll take you—"

"Clancy, fuck! No! Okay? No! You asked me and I said no!"

"What the fuck is your problem?" he asks. He doesn't ask it angrily. He asks it like—*Really. What is actually your problem, Molly?*

"Get out!" she screams.

She crosses the room and pushes him out of her doorway. I watch everything. I don't know what she's doing, I only know she is different. Something is different. Something has changed. Her body feels cold and shaky and I feel sick. I think she might throw up. I think—*Calm down, Molly. Really! Just calm down.*

She tries to slam the door, but Clancy sticks his foot in the way.

"Open the fucking door, Molly!" he screams. He pushes against the door and she kicks her foot against his foot but he's stronger. The door flies inward and smashes against the wall and Molly stumbles backward and catches her hip on the edge of the bureau. I feel her pain like it's my pain. Our pain. Tears spring to her eyes. Her vision blurs.

They face off. Molly is shaking. I feel her shaking.

"Go fuck yourself," Clancy says. He just looks at her.

And then she is different. She is still again. She is calm. She is breathing.

She says, "Do you ever wonder what it would be like without me?"

And he says, "No, really, Molly. You're an asshole. Fuck yourself."

She says, "Because someday, you'll find out. Maybe

someday you'll think back to this conversation and you'll remember it and you'll think . . ."

No, no, no, no.

No, wait.

Something is wrong. Something is going wrong. Something is unraveling. Something fragile has broken. Some string has snapped.

"What are you talking about?" Clancy asks.

"Don't worry. You'll all be better off without me," Molly says.

She pushes past him.

The pills are under her parents' vanity. He doesn't follow her. She puts them into her purse and then she goes downstairs and she takes a bottle of water from the fridge and then she slams the front door of the house and she runs across the yard to her car and she drives at exactly the speed limit. Her hands are white on the steering wheel but they are not shaking. And her mind—her mind is so quiet it's like she's not even there anymore. I can't hear her thinking, and I can always hear her thinking. I can always hear her thinking. But now it's like I am alone in her body just watching someone else drive us somewhere I have never been. Molly has never been here. I don't know what this place is.

It is October twenty-sixth. A Friday.

She drives to the warehouse and she parks in the empty parking lot and she gets out and stops only for a minute and looks up at this building and I still don't know what she's thinking but I'm scared. For the first time in my life, I am scared of her. I don't know what she's going to do. I don't know what she's planning.

She goes inside. She passes the homeless people and the junkies and she finds the fire that never goes out. The runaways don't even look up at her.

She pushes deeper into the warehouse and then I can feel her again. And then all of a sudden I can feel her again and she is happy. She is happy—a strange, lurching happiness that pulses and thrums through her body and settles in her fingers and the tip of her nose. And something else, there is something else. Relief. There is relief. There is stillness. There is calm.

She finds a small, abandoned room.

And that's where she stops.

She sits down on the floor of the warehouse and she takes the bottle of water out of her purse and she puts it in front of her and then she takes the bottle of sleeping pills and she puts them in front of her and then I think to myself—*oh.*

Oh, how could I have been so stupid?

She leans back against the wall and I can hear her again. I can hear what she's thinking and she's thinking—she's wondering—How long will it take me to die?

Will it be quick?

Will it be very painful?

She opens the bottle of pills and spills them out into her palm.

It will be easy, she thinks. It will be simple. I will just fall asleep.

And I think—I think, I wonder what I would have been like if I was normal. If I wasn't an alter, I mean. If I didn't have to share this body with her. With Molly.

It's not easy.

Every day I wake up when Molly wants to wake up. Every day I go to sleep when Molly is tired. I wear the clothes Molly wants to wear. I do my hair the way Molly wants to do her hair.

The movies I watch, the books I read.

But what little life I get—I want it. I like it.

And now here she is and she's going to ruin everything for me.

But—no. I won't let her.

I won't let her.

She unscrews the top of the water bottle and she holds the pills in her hands and she is trying to decide whether she should put them into her mouth one by one or all together.

And then all of sudden it is me.

It's me.

It's me and not Molly.

It's me and I'm holding the pills and I don't know how long I sit there just holding them but I can't move. It's been so long. It's been so long since I've taken over and it's like

I've forgotten how to move my body. Our body.

My body.

I don't know how long I'm there, but then someone sits down in front of me.

It's a boy. He's eating a cheese and tomato sandwich. He takes a big bite of the sandwich and then he holds it out to me and says, "Want some?"

And then I start crying.

And then he holds his hand out, palm up, and I dump all the pills into it and he takes the empty pill bottle from me and he uses his hand like a funnel and puts all the pills back into the bottle.

Then he takes the water bottle and holds it up and says, "Do you mind?" and I shake my head and he takes a big sip and he says, "Thanks." And he says, "What's your name?"

And I say, "Mabel."

And it is the first time I have ever introduced myself. It is the first time I have said my name out loud to a stranger.

And he says, "Mabel. I'm Lyle. It's nice to meet you."

And I say, "I wasn't going to do it."

And he says, "Oh. Okay."

And I say, "No really. I wasn't going to do it. I stopped her. I saved her life."

And I think—one day I will explain it to you. One day I will explain what I mean.

But right now. Right now I'm just so happy. Right now I'm alive. Right now I'm here. Right now I've saved

Molly's life. Because she would have done it. She was going to do it.

I heard her, and she was going to do it.

In the kitchen I peel an orange and eat wedge after wedge with deliberate care.

It's dark outside.

Mabel is quiet, for now.

I still can't feel her.

That day. That day.

I remember that day.

I mean—I remember that day now.

I didn't before.

It was all black.

Just another black spot in a year of black spots.

I remembered the fight with Clancy. And I remembered gathering the pills. And I even remembered getting into my car, but—

That was it. There was nothing after that.

But now . . .

Now it's all there.

I drove to the warehouse. I sat with the pills in my hand and I was about to put them in my mouth. I had decided—all at once. Put them into your mouth all at once and then take the water and swallow them. I had decided. I was about to do it.

I woke up hours later. Three hours, four hours. I was

sitting on my bed. I was sitting cross-legged on my bed with my homework spread out in front of me. I was halfway through a history assignment.

I was here. I was alive. I was still, somehow, alive.

My parents came into my bedroom.

My father was quiet. He stood near the door. My mother had been crying. I could tell; her eyes were red.

She said, "Molly. Hazel told us what you said."

She said, "Molly, do you really feel that way?"

She said, "How could you possibly feel that way?"

I was so confused. I wanted to ask her—Mom, how did I get here? Where have I been? What time is it and where have the last few hours gone and, yes. Yes, sure, I meant it. I meant it and I want to die and I tried to. I tried to, really, but somehow I ended up here.

The next day they asked for my help at the bookstore. We got into the minivan. They drove me to Alex's office.

He said, "Call me Alex. I'll call you Molly."

He said, "Do you sometimes feel hopeless?"

"Do you sometimes feel lost?"

"Do you sometimes feel like it's not worth it? None of it? Nothing at all?"

I said—yes. Yes to all of the above. Yes to everything. Yes, yes, yes.

TWENTY-ONE.

I wonder—How much was she like me?

Some nights did she stay up crying under the blankets we shared, wondering how just living and breathing and showering and brushing our teeth and combing our hair could be this fucking hard? Some nights did the walls of the house press in on her until her skull cracked and her brain squeezed together and her memories poured out of her ears? Some nights did she think, If I just had the guts to do it. If I just had the guts to take a bottle full of pills I would be okay. All these people, they would be better off without me.

I wonder how we are the same and I wonder how we are different.

But I guess I know already.

We're different because she didn't take the pills.

She didn't take the pills. She held them in her hands and I felt her gratitude—this rush of *happiness*—this blur of color as she took over our body and as she . . .

As she saved my life.

She saved my life.

And then Lyle. She gave the pills to Lyle. I guess she let him think he'd saved her. I guess he always thought he'd saved her, even though she told him. Even though she tried to explain to him—no, dummy. It wasn't you. It was me. It was me all along.

And she's probably gone now.

She's probably gone.

Upstairs, I take the photographs out of the shoe box and tape them to my wall in chronological order. Mabel as a baby. Mabel as a toddler. Mabel decorating a Christmas tree. Mabel riding a bike.

It's so obvious now.

This little girl, this isn't me. This isn't me at all.

And I think she's gone but then suddenly she isn't.

She's still here.

She has more to show me.

In the ambulance Mabel bursts out of me like a wave, and Lyle knows it's her but he's almost dead and all he can do is turn his eyes and look at her.

"Lyle," she says, "what the fuck did you do?"

"I'm sorry," he says.

"You can't die," she says. "You're my best friend. You can't leave me."

"You'll have Sayer," he says. Even in death his voice is full of bitterness.

"Don't do that now," she says. He's only seen her cry once before and her crying is what undoes him.

"I'm sorry," he says, "I just wanted to see you."

"Don't die," she whispers. "You can't die, okay?"

They want to put a tube into his mouth but he pushes them away. He says, "I'm so happy I met you."

They try to save his life.

In the hospital she calls Sayer with Lyle's cell phone and she says, "Sayer. There's been an accident. I'll call back in a few minutes but it won't be me. Don't call me Mabel."

When Sayer gets there, she comes out again and they sit holding each other in the private waiting room and it's Mabel who asks for the sedative. She can feel me unwinding inside her and she knows it's too much for me. The blood and the boy on the motorcycle and my sweater. She's the one who asks for the sedative.

Then in the graveyard.

Lyle's funeral.

They're lowering Lyle's body into the ground and Mabel takes Sayer's hand and he holds her and he cries and when he is done crying she says, "I can't do it anymore."

And I guess he's always known. Because he doesn't seem surprised.

"You should know her," she says. She holds his hand. "I won't be upset. She's like me, really. We're almost exactly the same."

"I want you," he insists. He tries to pull her closer.

"You never really had me," she says. "Just a small part Molly let you borrow."

"I had you," he says. "You're you. Mabel, I love you."

"You'll love her, too. You'll be good for her. You're kind."

Then Alex's office. Mabel takes over languidly, spreading herself throughout my body like she knows she better enjoy it because it might be the last time.

"Hey, Alex," she says. They get along better now.

"Thought I'd be seeing you."

"I have good news," she says.

"Oh?"

"It's almost time."

"What made you decide?"

"Molly. It's always Molly."

"How will you do it?"

"She'll tell you all about it."

"All right, Mabel. I trust you."

"So you've said."

She smiles but it's not real. It's not a real smile.

"Are you all right?" he says.

It has been six days since Lyle's death.

"Am I all right," she repeats. Her eyes blur momentarily out of focus and she inhales deeply through borrowed lungs. "Not really."

She goes home. She pretends to be me and nobody notices but Hazel. Hazel winks at her and Mabel winks back.

In my room, she pulls out a piece of paper. She sits down at my window seat and she curls her legs up and she writes very slowly. Very neat.

And then she gets up. She lifts up a corner of our mattress. And she slides the paper underneath.

She walks through the house like a ghost. Sometimes she thinks she would be better off without a body. Better off floating and diaphanous and thin.

She finds Hazel downstairs on the couch, watching TV. She goes and sits next to her and puts her head on her shoulder.

"What's wrong, Mabel?" Hazel says.

"Tell you later," she says.

"Want to watch TV?"

"Yeah. She has to call Alex when she wakes up. Don't let her forget."

"I won't."

They were always sisters.

When nobody knew her name, there was always Hazel.

• • •

In my bedroom I look at the photographs of Mabel.

It's like looking into a fun house mirror; the face reflected at once so similar and so distorted.

Looking at her face, I can almost feel her.

I get off the bed and stretch my legs. Lift up one corner of the mattress and feel around until I find it. The folded piece of paper.

I sit down at the window seat where she wrote it.

I can almost feel her. But she's leaving. She's melting back into me. Sealing the cracks in between us. Making us whole.

Molly,

I don't know how to start.

It's weird, writing this. It's almost like writing to myself.

For a long time, I thought we could go on sharing your body like we've done forever. When we were kids I learned to call myself Molly. I played with your brother and sister and they were my brother and sister, too. Your mom and dad were my mom and dad. I'm a lot like you, Molly, and I've learned to concentrate on our similarities. I was so good at acting like you.

And it was fine, really. I was able to accept a life living in your shadow. Because it meant a life.

Without you, I'd be nothing.

I know that.

And then you kind of ruined everything.

Sorry. It's the truth.

You were so sad. I get it. And you couldn't find a reason for your sadness, so you didn't know how to fix it. You didn't think there was any other way. So you stole the pills and you went to the warehouse and I remember that feeling. That feeling, that feeling—this happiness. You were so happy. You were finally going to do it.

But, Molly! What about me! If you died . . .

I'd die.

And I didn't want to die.

So I needed to save you.

I saved you.

I saved you and I met Lyle and I realized—

I realized I could have a life, too. I wanted a life, too. So I took yours. More and more, I started taking yours and I thought that was fair because you didn't even want it. You were going to get rid of it. You were going to give it away.

Maybe my life isn't much. But it's mine. And I wanted it.

And then I thought—I can make her better. I could make you better.

So I told Alex about me.

I like him.

He didn't make us take the drugs.

There are drugs that would have gotten rid of me. He threatened them, sure, but he didn't make us take them. And I promised him—I can make her better.

I told him how I saved you and I told him—just give me time.

And he did. All this time. For once in my life I had all this time.

And I had Lyle and Sayer.

And I liked that, but I knew it wouldn't last forever. It wouldn't work forever. I was coming out more and more, I was falling in love with Sayer, I was doing all these things I had watched you do over the years.

And then Lyle died.

We watched him die.

Fuck, it was so much harder for me, Molly. I loved him. We were friends.

But when he died . . .

I guess I realized—

What was I doing?

I wasn't trying to help you anymore.

I was trying to take over.

You have a great life, Molly.

I've always wondered what I was around for.

They say most alters develop after some sort of abuse.

Alex told me that. He told me we didn't really fit the mold.

*But now I think I understand it. Why you cre-
ated me.*

*That's hard for me to say. I don't like to think of
myself as being created. But it's true.*

I think you created me to help you.

*You would have killed yourself. And back then, I
thought I was saving myself but I was really saving
you. The one person I put before me. I guess I never
really had a choice, but in the end I was happy to
do it.*

So, Molly—be honest. Be happy.

You deserve to be whole.

You deserve to remember.

And you deserve to live.

—Mabel

Her handwriting is different from mine.

Smaller, careful letters formed with deliberate, even
strokes.

The way she writes my name is nothing like the way I
write my name.

Holding the letter, I know she's gone for good.

I don't feel like something has left me.

If I couldn't feel her, at least I thought I'd be able to
identify her absence. Identify some sort of hollow in the
space she occupied. I look in the mirror for pieces of my
face that resemble the girl in the photographs, but I find

nothing. She's gone.

Like identical twins. When you know what to look for, they cease being identical.

All I have is what she's left me with. The photographs. The letter. The memories. Sayer.

Everything she's kept hidden from me.

Everything that belonged to her and not to me.

Relinquished, now.

The final admission of guilt sitting in my hands. My fingers are shaking. Mabel's letter hums like a motorcycle engine.

The warehouse.

Lyle.

I can remember holding the pills in my hand and I can remember giving them to Lyle as if I was the one who had done it.

She stole my death from me. My suicide. She's gone now and I'm the one forced to stay and live here without her.

If she hadn't shown up in the warehouse that day, where would I be?

I would have taken the pills.

I would have done it.

And knowing—

That's a fucking awful feeling.

TWENTY-TWO.

Good days, bad days—and more often than not—days that fall somewhere in the middle.

Sometimes it's easy and sometimes it's impossible and sometimes I am walking down the hallway between the bathroom and my bedroom and I don't even know how I got here. I don't know how I ended up here. I don't know how I wake up every day and get out of bed and take a shower and brush my teeth and put one foot in front of the other.

It's like sometimes I can't remember. It's like sometimes I do things, I do all the things I'm supposed to do, but on the inside I'm just barely functioning. I am just barely managing. I'm just faking it. I am only faking it—*this life*—and one day someone is going to look at me and they are going to know and then maybe they will put me away somewhere because I don't deserve any of it. Mabel is gone but I think she should have stayed and I think I should have been the one to fade away, disappear, sink into the depths of our body, into a tiny wedge where no one would ever, ever find me. She could have Sayer again. She is happier than I am; she deserves this more than I do.

One by one I take the pictures down and I put them back into the shoe box. I lay the letter on top and I close the box and I slide it under my bed. Hardly a ceremonious burial, but I don't know what else to do with them.

All I keep thinking—the one image that keeps replaying over and over in my head—is me in the warehouse. I can feel Mabel then, I can feel her like a spring, quivering and watching me like—Molly, please don't do it. Please, please, please don't do it. I can see the handful of pills in my hand and I can feel this moment. I can identify the exact moment before I do it—before I *will* do it—and that is the moment Mabel takes over and it is the first time she has done it like this. She has been around forever but this is the first time she has done something so purposefully. She has decorated a Christmas tree with my family and she has watched TV with Hazel and she has ridden a bike in our driveway, but she has always kept quiet. She has always gone unnoticed.

I can feel her now. I remember. I remember her decision. She saved my life and in return she took a year away from me and now she's gone and I want to bring her back.

This is too hard. This is too much. I never wanted this and besides—

You were so much better at it.

You were happier; you were prettier; you were taller. The way you held your shoulders and the way you wrote my name.

Wednesday morning I'm early to school; Erie and Luka are waiting for me at my locker.

Erie scowls when she sees me.

I've been avoiding them.

Monday and Tuesday I actually pretended to be sick. I pretended to have a sore throat just so I wouldn't have to talk to them.

But now Erie is scowling and Luka is smirking and I have to say to myself—These are your friends, Molly. These are your friends. You have to talk to them now.

"Hey," Luka says when I get close enough.

Erie scowls more.

Do I know how many text messages she sent me yesterday, Molly?

Do I need a lesson in how to work a phone, Molly?

Because she'd be happy to show me. Really. It's no problem at all.

"I'm sorry," I say. Luka steps behind me and puts his

arms around my shoulders. He rests his chin on my head.

"You seem weird," he says. "Are you weird?"

"I'm fine," I say.

"Obviously you're not fine," Erie says.

"Really, I'm fine."

"Don't you even want to know what was so important?" she says.

"What was so important with what?"

"With *me*, Molly. What was so important with *me*."

"Yes. Definitely. What was so important with you?"

"I only wanted to tell you I broke up with Paul."

"Paul?" I say. "Who the hell is Paul?"

She leans in closer. Like a secret, she whispers it into my ear.

"Carbon," she says.

"I knew that wasn't his name," Luka says. "Molly, didn't I say that? Didn't I say that wasn't his name?"

"He was a little off," Erie says. Then she remembers she's supposed to be scowling and she looks at me and says, "To be honest, I could have used a friend, but somebody doesn't know how to work a cell phone."

"I know how to use a cell phone," Luka says.

"Not you, Luka," she says, rolling her eyes.

I find it. I dig around in my backpack until I feel my cell phone and I pull it out and I hold it up so she can see.

Dead. I am triumphant. It is dead.

Erie shakes her head sadly, rendered speechless. How

anyone could let their phone die, she will never know.

Luka pulls away. He leans against my locker. He puts his hand on Erie's shoulder.

"There, there," he says. "Look on the bright side."

"Now you don't have to find a girlfriend?" Erie guesses.

"Exactly."

"What about you?" Erie asks, turning back to me. "What about Sayer?"

I'm about to answer when she stops me. She puts her hand on my cheek. She pokes me with her index finger. Luka looks at her and then looks at me and then looks back at her and then looks at me, and then something changes in his face.

"What?" I say. "What is it?"

"Luka's right; you look weird. Something's different," Erie says.

Oh.

"Oh?"

"You do. I told you," Luka confirms.

"Like—how?" I ask.

"Oh, Molly," Erie says.

"What?" I say.

"You don't have to say anything," Erie says.

"Oh," I say.

Erie shrugs. Luka puts his hand on the top of my head and the bell rings and they leave me standing alone because, I don't know—maybe they can tell. Maybe they know she's gone. Or maybe they just know that sometimes I want to be alone. Sometimes it's just—

Sometimes it's impossible.

Talking to people is impossible.

Mabel was always better at that than I was.

I lean against my locker.

The hallway's empty.

And when I see him near the water fountain, I get it.

I live in a small town. Everyone knows everyone. That's why I know that four years ago Chris Jennings hooked a hose to the gas pipe of his car and ran it into his taped-up window.

Bret's brother.

He was in his first year of college.

I've never thought about him before but I always knew—

I always knew he looked at me strangely. Bret. I always knew I felt weird around him.

I've never given his brother a second thought. I was in middle school when it happened.

We all have our reasons to be sad.

They're different but they're also the same.

Bret gets a drink of water from the fountain and when he stands up I'm right behind him.

"Molly, hey," he says.

"Hey, Bret," I say.

"How's it going?"

"Fine. Thanks. Listen—I wanted to tell you I'm sorry

about your brother. It's been a long time, I know. But I don't think I've ever said it."

I could have slapped him. His face drains of color and refills blotchily and he doesn't breathe for forty seconds. I count.

But then he hugs me.

It's a real hug.

He hugs me in the hallway; and when he pulls away, he looks at me like I'm something special, I guess. Something to be celebrated. I don't know if that's true but it's a nice feeling anyway.

"I've heard things," he says. "I don't know how much is true."

"Probably all of it," I say, smiling.

"Is there anything I can do? Anything, ever? I mean, are you . . ."

The unsaid word is *okay*.

Are you okay, Molly?

Are you still sad, Molly?

Do you still sometimes wish it would all just painlessly, easily, go away?

I laugh and it fills up the hallway with sound. "I'm here," I say.

That's sort of all I'm certain of. I'm here. I'm alive. I did not take a handful of pills in a dirty, empty warehouse. I will never know how long it would have taken me to die. I will never know if it would have hurt. I'm here.

"That's good," he says. And he says it so earnestly that I feel myself blush—a long, slow blush that sets my face on fire. Bret touches my hand and I smile and then I shrug.

And then I say, "See you around."

And he says, "Sure, yeah," and he squeezes my hand, and he walks away and I watch him go until he turns a corner and disappears. And then I watch the space he used to fill and I can't imagine not being here. I can't imagine not standing here. Sometimes I wish I had never been born, sometimes I feel like I can't breathe, sometimes I cry for no reason, and sometimes I can't fall asleep, but sometimes— now, now, here—I can't imagine ever being anything but grateful.

In the parking lot of Alex's building, I sit in my car and I wonder what I will say.

What will I say to him?

I imagine him in session with someone else, taking notes or sitting on his desk with his hands folded in his lap.

"I've never really been honest with you," I'll say. That's what I'll say.

"Honest about what?"

Honest about anything. Honest about what I'm feeling, about how hopeless everything seems, about how my parents have to hide the migraine pills just so I won't take too many. I'll tell him Mabel's gone and he'll ask me how my body feels without her. Is there more room now? Do I feel like two separate pieces of my personality have fused together? Do you feel any different, Molly? Any different at all?

Fuck, Alex. I don't know.

In the waiting room, I leaf through magazines until the man before me gets out of his session. His eyes are rimmed with red; he doesn't look at me.

I wait the five minutes until Alex pokes his head out of his office. He smiles at me.

"Hi, Molly," he says.

"Hey, Alex."

In his office he lowers the blinds halfway and I wait until he's sitting before I talk. He sits on the edge of his desk and then he looks at me and I wait for him to say it. I know he's going to say it because he looks at me for too long with his eyes almost squinted like he's trying to figure it out.

"Is she . . ."

"Yeah," I say.

"Are you okay?"

"Yeah," I say. I reconsider. "No." I reconsider again. "Sort of."

He smiles. "Want to talk about it?"

"I don't understand," I say.

"What don't you understand, Molly?"

It's like—

Sometimes you're watching TV and suddenly you can't

watch TV anymore. Suddenly you can't do anything except go to your room and shut the door and sit on the carpet with the lights off, your hands over your face so your sister can't hear you crying.

Sometimes it is unbearable. Impossible.

"I don't know what's wrong with me."

He nods. He says, "Tell me about that day."

"What day?" I ask.

But I know what day. Of course I know what day.

So I say, "I was going to do it."

And he says, "I know."

"I mean—I was really going to do it. I wanted to do it. Still, sometimes . . ."

"Sometimes you wish—"

"That I had. Yeah. Sometimes I wish I had."

"But not all the time?"

"Not all the time."

"How about now?" he asks. "How do you feel now?"

"Now?" I pause.

How do I feel now? I know how I felt a few minutes ago and I know how I felt when I talked to Bret, but I don't know if I know how I feel now.

Or maybe I do. Maybe I feel—

"I feel lonely," I say. "Without her. I feel lonely without her."

"Why?" he asks.

"Because she . . ."

Because she saved my life. She didn't let me do it. She gave the pills away.

Alex leans forward. He touches my knee. I look up at him.

"You do know—you do realize, Molly—that you made her. You created her. Do you understand what that means?"

I understand what it means but I want to hear him say it, so I shake my head. I shake my head and I wait for him.

"It means—you don't have to feel lonely. She hasn't really gone anywhere. And it means—"

"It means somewhere, I'm okay," I interrupt.

It means somewhere inside me, I'm not sad. Somewhere, I am fixed. Somewhere, I am happy.

It's hidden. It's lost. I just have to find it. I don't know how I will find it, but at least I know it's real. It is inside me, somewhere.

I just have to figure it out.

I just have to know where to look.

He's leaning against my car again, minus the umbrella and plus a stack of spiral-bound notebooks he's clutching with both his hands. Mabel's notebooks. He holds them out to me when I get close enough, and I take them and I unlock the car and put them into the backseat.

"You have this creepy habit of showing up in parking lots," I say.

Sayer laughs. He shrugs his shoulders. "Let's go for a walk," he says.

He takes my hand and we start down the road, leaving our cars outside Alex's building.

We walk down the road toward the beach, winding our way down the twisting path until we reach the white shore.

It's cold here. The breeze from the water blows my hair around my face and I pull it back into a ponytail. Sayer watches me. He's still watching me for signs of her.

But she's gone.

She has to be gone because this was the only time I could feel her.

Being with Sayer. I could feel her reaching for him. The magnet feeling I couldn't explain. I think Sayer was the only person she ever really loved.

And he must have loved her, too, because he's searching my face for her and he takes my hand in his hand like he'll find her in my fingers.

"What does it feel like?" he asks.

Everyone wants to know what it feels like, but it doesn't feel like anything. She was here and she is gone and she was never really here and she will never really be gone. She was me—just a part of me I refused to acknowledge, a part of me I didn't know how to reach.

I shrug. "I miss Lyle."

I don't know what makes me think of him. Except they look so similar, the brothers, and in the fading light of the beach, if I squint my eyes and make them go blurry, Sayer could be Lyle. Lyle could be alive.

"Yeah," Sayer says. "Me, too."

I woke up in my car and I didn't know how I got there but I was driving and he was following me. In my rearview mirror I watched him swerve in and out of traffic and I watched him run a red light and I watched the truck hit his back tire and I lost him over my roof and then he was there again, in front of me. And something made me pull his helmet off, something made me hold his head in my lap, something made me hold him while he bled and died and he asked me to pretend.

"At least pretend," he'd said. "I need you to pretend."

Something made me stay with him, even then, when I didn't know who he was.

"Hey," Sayer says.

We walk along the water's edge. It's cold and it's windy and I lean into him. He puts his arm around my shoulders.

"Hey," I say.

"I don't want . . . ," he says, but then he stops. I pull away from him and he doesn't look at me. He looks somewhere past me, out over the water.

"What?" I ask.

"I don't want to lose you again."

And I'm about to say—but that wasn't me. She wasn't me. I'm not her—but then there's a voice in my head and it's not mine. It sounds like me and anyone else in the world, they would mistake it for me. They would think it was me.

But it's not me. It's not me, really. It's almost me. It's half of me.

It's just—

Sometimes I get so sad I think my mind will rip and I will split into two separate people. I will keep all my sadness in one part of me. I will keep all my happiness in another.

We will share a body; she will give herself a name. My sister will like her.

She'll sew herself up when she thinks I'm ready.

She'll write me a letter. Instructions for how to live without her.

You deserve to be whole.

You deserve to remember.

You deserve to live.

This voice in my head, it's telling me he'll be good for me. It's telling me he's kind. It's telling me I should give him this one chance. Just do this. Let yourself be happy.

There's this voice, but I don't have to listen to it. I can turn it off. I don't have to hear her anymore.

I can do this part by myself.

ACKNOWLEDGMENTS

This book wouldn't be a book without the help, encouragement, guidance, and love of many, many people.

First and foremost—to my parents, who welcomed me back into their home and defended me against those who questioned my decisions. I wouldn't have been able to write this without their support and generosity.

To my brothers, of course, and my sisters-in-law. To Ric for giving me a home in Brooklyn when I felt like I didn't have a home anywhere, for always feeding me, and for buying me the Chronicles of Narnia when I was younger. To Colby for bringing me around the world, for coming to see me in Edinburgh, and for always giving the most thoughtful, honest advice. To Brittany for being my first fake sister, for always listening to my next big idea, and for finding Milo. To Nicole for her openness, her warmth, and for making me feel welcome wherever she is.

To RHA—he was important and he is missed. He was the first person to ask me straight: *What are you* doing *with your life?* He made me rethink everything.

To Colleen, who taught me how to write a query letter and showed me how the literary world worked and who answered all my relentless questions—thank you.

To Dr. Jeffrey Lazar for early medical answers and for being the first person I told it to: I'm thinking about writing a book.

To my agent, Wendy Schmalz, for her patience and honesty. To my editor, Sarah Dotts Barley, for her passion and commitment. Two such important people; I hope I know them for a very long time.

To the magical people at HarperCollins who helped make Molly the best she could be: Alison Lisnow, Christina Colangelo, Alexei Esikoff, and Alison Klapthor.

To the rest of my family and friends for their support and interest and love. To MMW for once hearing the same thunder as me, to AJS for once carrying a French tote bag, to TAM for once stomping through the snow, and to SDA for once flying halfway around the world to see me. WP, you are cared for.

To all those fighting for better mental health awareness and treatment in America. You are heroes, and this book was inspired by you.

To all those who supported me through my own struggle with depression and mental illness. That was the darkest time in my life, and without them I would never have made it out.

And finally, to all those struggling with their own melancholy (as Molly's mother would call it)—there will come a change for the better. You deserve to be whole. You deserve to live.

SOMETIMES YOU HAVE TO GET LOST BEFORE YOU CAN BE FOUND. . . .

Keep reading for a sneak peek at Katrina Leno's charming and imaginative new novel.

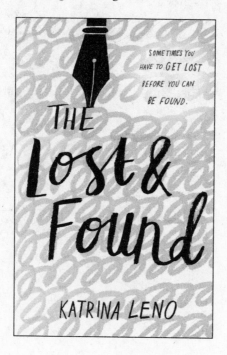

ONE
Frances

My grandparents' mailbox is shaped like a tiny replica of their house.

The bay window in the front, the glass-walled solarium on the side, the second-floor balcony off the master bedroom—everything is miniature and perfect and done in 1:12 scale.

My grandmother is strangely proud of this mailbox, probably because she paid a fortune to have it custom made fifteen years ago. I've seen her with a tiny can of paint and the most delicate paintbrush, repainting the shutters so they stay shiny and perfect. I've seen her pulling miniature leaves out of gutters the size of straws.

It was big and faintly ostentatious and kind of a work of art, in a weird way, and I'd been standing in front of it for five or six minutes, trying to get up the courage to open the tiny garage door, which is where the mail went.

I hadn't checked the mail in years.

The mailbox, while impressive, has always been a source of unlikely danger.

Just a few days after I moved into my grandparents' house on the Miles River in Maryland, my grandfather caught a black widow spider spinning a web in between a bill for my grandmother's subscription to *Good Housekeeping* and the morning paper.

He trapped the spider in a coffee canister and paraded it around the house loudly, making a big show of it. I asked to see it but was denied.

"Well then, why did you bring it in the house?" I asked.

"Just giving it a little taste of the good life before I set it free."

"Where are you going to set it free?" I pressed him. I extended one hand to touch the side of the coffee canister, and he swatted me away.

"Don't worry," he said. "Far away from here."

He set the canister down on the kitchen table while he got his coat on. I watched from the doorway.

"Are you sure I can't see it?" I asked.

"I'm sure," he said. "And you know what? You better not get the mail anymore, Frannie. These things are like pigeons. They can always find their way home."

I had no great desire to prove my bravery by risking a bite from a black widow spider, so I avoided the mailbox after that.

For five years I walked a wide, careful circle around it. For five years I checked underneath my pillow and in between my sheets for relatives of the black widow that had once famously moved into the nicest mailbox-house in Easton.

But as warnings often do, that one grew stale.

And after five years (and six minutes) spent gathering my courage, I opened the miniature garage door and withdrew the mail from inside.

The letter I was expecting hadn't come yet.

Bills, a flyer from our local grocery store, a few credit card companies begging for my grandparents' business. Nothing interesting.

I put everything back in the mailbox, but one letter slipped out and fell to the ground. It was addressed to Mr. and Mrs. Jameson, and when I picked it up I read the return address, stamped slightly crooked at the corner: the Easton Valley Rest and Recuperation Center for the Permanently Unwell.

But no—

Was one of my grandparents sick? Could they be keeping something like that from me?

I tore it open, terrified, and scanned it quickly.

It was a bill for a coffin.

I read it again, confused, slowly, trying to understand the words typed out in some small, precise font.

It was addressed to my grandparents.

My brain picked out bits and pieces, unable to process the whole thing at once.

Dear Mr. and Mrs. Jameson,
We have received your initial down payment.
Coffin.
Remaining balance.
Our deepest sympathies.
Please call if you would like to discuss payment plan options.

My grandparents had bought the coffin at a discounted rate. They had paid two hundred dollars of the fourteen hundred owed. It was originally two thousand.

It was a fourteen-hundred-dollar coffin.

For my mother.

But my mother had moved to Florida five years ago. My mother had taken the remainder of our money and left me to live with Grandpa Dick and Grandma Doris.

My mother wasn't dead. My mother hadn't died. And my mother had certainly never been at the Easton Valley Rest and Recuperation Center for the Permanently Unwell.

Unless . . .

Suddenly I wasn't so sure there had ever actually been a spider in our mailbox.

I don't have a lot of memories of my childhood.

My therapist said this was normal, probably some form of repression coupled with post-traumatic stress.

The first thing I can remember is an ice-cream cone.

My father bought me an ice-cream cone from an ice-cream truck. He handed me the cone, and I dropped it on the ground. I was maybe three or four. My canvas shoes had tiny giraffes printed on them, and the ice cream splattered on the toes.

He wouldn't buy me another cone.

I won't lie: I wish my first memory was a nicer one. I wish I remembered eating cake at my third birthday party or petting a dog for the first time or going to a park with my mom and being pushed a little too high on the swings.

But I guess we don't get to choose those kinds of things.

After the ice-cream cone incident, I remember some birthday parties, a first bike ride, some memorable Christmases, some blizzards, and some heat waves. But nothing really substantial sticks out until I was nine years old.

That is when my father either tried to kill me (if you listen to my mother) or just lost his temper but did NOT try to kill me (if you listen to my father).

• • •

What happened was my father and my mother had an argument.

The reason for the argument is not important. Who was right and who was wrong is not important. The beginning of the argument is not important.

The end of the argument is the important part, because that is when my parents wouldn't stop yelling and so I started yelling, at the top, top, top of my lungs until my voice cracked and my parents had to stop yelling at each other and start yelling at me, trying everything they could to shut me up until finally my father uncapped his fountain pen, strode across the living room, and stabbed me with his right hand. Just above and to the left of my belly button.

When my father let go of the pen, it stuck out of my stomach at a right angle. I was wearing a pink-and-white bikini. In another scenario, it would have been funny.

My mother screamed.

My father put his hands up like, *Oh shit, I fucked up,* and he backed away from me slowly.

I watched the blood leak out from around the pen, and the blood was almost black. Was it blood or ink? I couldn't tell which was which. It was all the same rich, thick darkness.

It leaked out of me in a thin river that filled my belly button and stained my bathing suit bottoms.

My mother screamed again and yanked the pen out of

my stomach (which you are not supposed to do, we later found out).

In the hospital after it happened, my mother held my hand before they wheeled me into surgery. I was crying and my stomach hurt and my clothes were ruined but my mother's face was incredibly calm, almost smug.

"You're gonna be okay, Heph," she said. She pronounced it like *Hef.* I generally discouraged the nickname, but I tolerated it then because I thought I might die in surgery and this would be the last time I ever saw her. And I didn't want the last time I ever saw her to be marred with an argument about my name.

Regarding my name, this is how I got it:

My mother requested the maximum dosage of painkillers and a birthing doctor who was notoriously lax with the meds.

She fell asleep halfway through a push. They had to wake her up and remind her where she was.

"I was having a really nice dream," she said.

"You're about to have a really nice baby," the doctor said.

"I want to call her Hephaestus," she announced.

"That's a terrible name," my father said. "I thought we were calling her Margaret."

"It was in my dream. Just now. It's Hephaestus or nothing."

"What kind of a name is that? It's a terrible name."

"I heard it somewhere," she said.

Hephaestus was the Greek god of metalworking. I'm not sure why it just suddenly occurred to her.

"We are not calling our baby Hephaestus," my father said.

"You have to push now," the doctor said. "I'm sorry to interrupt, but you have to push."

"I hate the name Margaret, and I hate you!" my mother said.

"Pushing now, naming later," the doctor said.

My mother pushed.

I slid out of my mother's body and into the doctor's waiting, bloody hands. He handed the scissors to my father and then looked at him expectantly.

"Hmm?" my father said.

The doctor looked from me to my umbilical cord and then back to my father again.

"Oh," my father said. "Okay. How important is it that I do it?"

The scissors were removed from my father's hands. A nurse cut my umbilical cord, the sacred rope that served as an in-between from the world inside to the world outside.

The tether that linked me to my mother. My mother who promptly fell asleep again as soon as I was free of her.

I know all of this is exactly how it happened because my father brought a video camera into the birthing room. He pressed Record and then left the camera on a table. The lens was pointed at my mother's vagina.

My father named me while my mother was sleeping. He had been prepared to call me Margaret but he settled for naming me after himself. Frances.

When my mother woke up, she threatened to put me back inside her if Hephaestus wasn't at least my middle name. She pointed out that was a perfectly fair compromise.

My father pointed out you couldn't actually put a baby back inside a womb, but he obliged her request.

It's nice to meet you.

I am:

Frances Hephaestus Jameson.

My mother got full custody in the divorce proceedings—I mean, duh, obviously—because my father was in jail serving a twelve-month sentence for stabbing me with a pen.

For a while it was great.

My mother and I were thick as thieves, united against this common enemy (my attacker!), spending the settlement money like it was a lot more than it actually was, buying new clothes and new shoes and growing our hair long enough to wear braids down to our butts (in her post-divorce state, my mother had reverted to her earlier hippie inclinations), and doing interviews for local news programs.

People were really interested in my story for a number of reasons, but probably mostly because my mother cried buckets of tears on camera while still managing to look completely flawless. Her mascara never ran. Her hair was always shiny. Her eyes were always bright. I think people were just truly interested in how she managed it.

My mother was present and invested in my life. She was a best friend, a comrade, a partner-in-crime. We traveled around the country together in one of those very old VW vans that always smelled faintly of dirt. I felt like I was really a part of something. We were a team, my mother and I.

Only she turned out to be just as crazy as my father. And then it wasn't so great.

Then one day I got off the school bus and it wasn't my mother waiting for me. Instead, my grandparents stood huddled underneath an umbrella (it wasn't raining, but Grandpa Dick opened an umbrella the moment the sky turned even the slightest bit gray).

"Oh, hi," I said.

"You tell her," Grandpa Dick said.

"Honey, we have something to tell you," Grandma Doris said.

"It's about your mother," Grandpa added.

"I thought you wanted me to tell her?"

"So tell her."

I waited. Grandpa Dick turned around. Grandma Doris put her hand on my cheek.

"Oh, Frances," she said. "We love you so much."

• • •

After my father stabbed me, after my mother pulled the fountain pen out of my stomach even though you are not supposed to do that, after I pressed my fingers into my stomach to try and stop the bleeding, after I asked everybody to please stop staring at me and call an ambulance, after the ambulance ride and the hospital and a couple surgeries and a ton of X-rays later, a doctor came into the room with a funny sort of smile on his face and said, "Okay. Here's the thing."

And that is how I found out that the nib of the fountain pen had broken off and stayed inside me, and this is the most interesting part of the whole thing, in my opinion: they never found it.

Now I set off metal detectors. They pat me down. They get the metal detecting wand and wave it over me.

Every time, it beeps in a different place.

Since then, I have always lost things. My grandparents called me forgetful, my aunt Florence called me absent-minded, my uncle Irvine said I was preoccupied.

But that wasn't it. I wasn't forgetful or absentminded or preoccupied.

I didn't lose things.

Things left me.

ALSO FROM

Katrina Leno

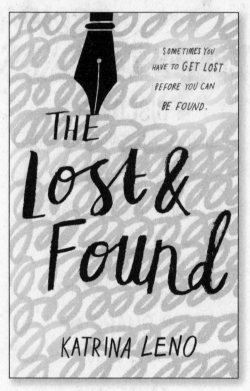

SOMETIMES YOU
HAVE TO GET LOST
BEFORE YOU CAN
BE FOUND.

THE

Lost &
Found

KATRINA LENO

THE STORY OF TWO TEENS ON OPPOSITE SIDES OF THE COUNTRY
SEARCHING FOR ANSWERS—AND EACH OTHER.